Joanna fel[t] awareness a[s] towards Mat[t]

In the semi-darkness it was difficult to see more than the outline of his face. But she sensed him breathing, felt the beat of his pulse under her thumb as it curled against his wrist.

Matt tightened his grip on her fingers, feeling her respond. He wanted to draw her closer, much closer, bury his face in her hair, breathe in her perfume. His throat worked as he swallowed. 'Joanna…'

Suddenly their absorption with one another was shattered as starkly as the crack of a rifle in an arctic wilderness, with the sound of a piercing cry of anguish.

Leah Martyn's writing career began at age eleven, when she wrote the winning essay in the schoolwork section of a country show. As an adult, success with short stories led her to try her hand at a longer work. With her daughter training to be a Registered Nurse, the highs and lows of hospital life struck a chord, and writing Medical Romances™ liberally spiked with humour became a reality. Home is with her husband in semi-rural Queensland, Australia. Her hobbies include an involvement with live theatre and relaxing on the beach with a good book.

Recent titles by the same author:

THE DOCTOR'S MARRIAGE
THE ER AFFAIR

THE FAMILY PRACTITIONER

BY
LEAH MARTYN

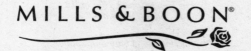

First published in Great Britain 2002
Harlequin Mills & Boon Limited,
Eton House, 18-24 Paradise Road, Richmond, Surrey TW9 1SR

© Leah Martyn 2002

ISBN 0 263 83428 X

Set in Times Roman 10½ on 12¼ pt.
03-0203-43067

Printed and bound in Spain
by Litografia Rosés, S.A., Barcelona

CHAPTER ONE

'A NUDE calendar!' Joanna felt her jaw drop.

Flushing slightly, Jason dipped his head, slotting the last of his textbooks into his back pack. 'It'll be cool.'

Joanna's mouth tilted wryly. 'Well, it would be, if you've nothing on.'

'Come on, Mum,' Jason wheedled. 'It's the only way to raise big bucks fast. The club needs a canteen and Matt says all the abseiling gear's stuffed as well.'

Matt says, Matt says. Frustratedly, Joanna speared both hands through her thick dark hair, sending the stylishly cut bob into disarray. The words had begun to sound like a mantra, repeated with monotonous regularity by Jason for the past couple of months.

In fact, ever since Dr Matthew McKellar had arrived in Glenfield and taken over the old gym with the intention of revamping it into a sporting centre-cum-sports-medicine clinic.

And, of course, if it had anything to do with sports, Jason wanted to be involved, she thought.

'Well, is it OK?' Hefting his bag over one shoulder, Jason's look was hopeful. 'The rest of the guys are cool about it.'

Joanna sighed. Why was nothing ever simple? 'You're *sixteen*, Jase. I need to know more about it.'

'Matt says it'll be tasteful—'

Joanna rolled her eyes. 'Let me think about it.'

5

'I have to know by the weekend—'

'And I have to think about it.' Joanna was firm. Getting up from the kitchen table, she wound a hug around his shoulders. 'Now go,' she added gently, 'or you'll miss your bus. And it's my late evening at the surgery,' she reminded him.

'No worries. I'll heat up the last of the lasagne.' He grinned winningly, as if he already knew he had her onside. 'Thanks, Mum.' Dropping a brief kiss on the top of her head, he shot out the door.

'And make a salad!' she called after him. Without turning, he lifted a hand in acknowledgement and Joanna shook her head. He was maturing so fast, miles taller than her now, and showing every sign of turning into a fine adult.

And that was all she'd ever wanted for him. Watching him jog down the path and vault the low front fence, her dark eyes were wistful.

Then she turned abruptly, as if coming to a decision. Her first appointment wasn't until ten this morning and she had no house calls listed. Quickly putting the kitchen to rights, she went through to her bedroom.

Nude calendars indeed! It was time she found out just where this Dr Matthew McKellar was coming from.

Annoyance was still simmering as she pulled on the rust-flecked trousers and camel shirt she normally wore to the surgery. Closing the zip at the waistband of her trousers, she brought her head up, almost startling herself with her own reflection in the full-length mirror.

Joanna'a spirits sagged. She looked so...*ordinary*.

Her hairstyle and make-up were, of necessity, simple and took no more than a cursory five or six minutes in front of the mirror each morning. And so what? she rationalised. Even if she had time, she had no wish to start preening. A month ago she'd turned thirty-five, for heaven's sake!

Suddenly, her expression firmed. Like it or not, if she was going to tackle Matthew McKellar about the ethics of what he was proposing, she needed power-dressing.

'I don't believe I'm doing this!' she muttered, and began hastily to divest herself of the clothes she'd just put on.

She slid back the door on the fitted wardrobe, taking only seconds to select the outfit that had been her present to herself on her recent birthday. Carefully, she laid the purple tweed trousers and matching pure wool sweater across the bed.

She took her time dressing and then looked in the mirror, pleased with what she saw. She loved winter. The coolness of the season allowed one to dress with much more elegance, she decided, slipping her feet into neat little ankle boots.

And now for the pièce de résistance. Her heart skipped. The softly fitting jacket had been a sheer extravagance but worth every cent. Her fingers stroked lovingly along the lapels of the lushly toned aubergine leather. Heavens, she felt almost sexy...

Disbelieving of her wayward thoughts—thoughts she hadn't had in years—she quickly deepened her shade of lipstick and slid an oval silver bangle over her left wrist.

She allowed herself a final look in the mirror, disconcerted to see someone she didn't quite know…

In the kitchen, she slipped back into her parenting role, scribbling a note for Jason to put out the garbage bin for collection. The salutary reminder of her real world curved a wry smile around her mouth. Then, hefting her medical bag, she collected her keys from the hall table and made her way outside to the carport.

Joanna drove her sporty little sedan through the leafy suburb towards Glenville's central business district, not for the first time thanking providence for directing her to this pleasant regional city in Queensland.

She'd arrived here two years ago with a moody teenager in tow, hoping she'd done the right thing in coming north from Canberra for this job in the Strachan Clinic where she now worked as a family practitioner.

And it had worked out well, she considered. Set free from two sets of over-indulgent grandparents, Jason had become self-reliant, even holding down a Saturday job at the local supermarket and scholastically doing well at the boys' college where he was enrolled.

And yet… A tiny frown etched itself between her brows. Just lately she'd noticed subtle changes in him. Were they tied in with his involvement at the sports centre? She shook her head. This wasn't the time to begin making snap judgements but, quite obviously, it was time she met Dr Matthew McKellar.

Almost as if she expected a clash of temperaments, her stomach muscles tightened as she turned into the rear car park of the white stuccoed building from where Dr McKellar conducted his business.

Her medical case would be safe enough in her boot, she decided, hitching up her plain leather shoulder bag and dropping her keys into the side pocket. Turning from closing the door of the car, she took a moment to look around her.

Although it was still reasonably early, there were already a number of cars in the parking area. She felt undecided, rolling her bottom lip between her teeth. Perhaps she should have done him the professional courtesy of making an appointment...

Her shoulders lifted in a deep, controlling breath, sudden nerves sitting heavily on her butterflies as she moved across the car park towards the covered walkway that ran down the side of the building.

Joanna had no idea what to expect. Would there be bodies pumping iron all over the place? An atmosphere of male exclusivity? It had been years since she'd been near a gymnasium. These days her only concession towards fitness was the occasional weekend game of tennis with her colleagues from the practice.

Well, here goes, she thought, releasing the single button on her leather jacket before pushing open the heavy plate-glass front door.

She'd unconsciously braced herself for nothing like the reality, she thought, turning in a space that was light, warm and welcoming. She felt the calming atmosphere immediately and realised it was being enhanced by the unmistakable, uplifting sound of a Vivaldi string ensemble that was being piped throughout the building.

Cautiously, Joanna raised her head, her gaze suddenly uncertain as it travelled along the curved staircase leading up to a gallery floor. She swallowed unevenly. She'd guess that's where he had his office—

'Hi! Can I help? You look a bit lost.'

Joanna spun round and looked straight into a pair of the most startling blue eyes she had ever seen. She blinked, feeling a jolt of something that rocked her to the core, and stammered, 'Um, I—I'm looking f-for Dr McKellar.'

'You've found him.' The man held out his hand and she took it, feeling her own engulfed by the masculine firmness. He raised a darkish brow. 'And you are?'

'Oh!' Joanna was completely off balance, flushing under his warm regard. 'Joanna Winters. I don't have an appointment,' she added jerkily. 'I, uh, just wondered if I could have a word about my son, Jason.'

Matthew McKellar was taken aback. The lady looked hardly more than a teenager herself. And she was lovely... He felt the oddest twist in the pit of his stomach. Almost defensively, he lifted a hand, thrusting his fingers through the short strands of his dark hair. 'Better come on up, then.' He thumbed across at the staircase and promptly led the way.

He took the stairs with a swift athleticism and Joanna followed, her gaze absorbing the six-foot length of him. He was clad in track pants and a white T-shirt delineating a sleek grouping of muscles underneath and bearing a logo that exhorted, MAKE ANOTHER HEART THROB. GIVE BLOOD.

Innovative, she approved. And heaven knew, there was always an urgent need for blood donors.

A bit warily, she stepped over the threshold of his office and looked around. It was upmarket but unpretentious, with linen pull-down blinds at the windows and unobtrusive pearl-grey paintwork on the walls. She made a thoughtful little moue with her bottom lip, intrigued to see there was no desk as such. Instead, a round table and chairs were grouped in a conversational-type setting near the window.

'Have a seat.' McKellar pulled out one of the softly upholstered chairs. 'Would you like juice, coffee?' He smiled then, the action softening his slightly hawk-like features.

Joanna's return smile faltered. 'Coffee might be nice, thanks.' And at least it would give her something to do with her hands, she reflected ruefully, watching him take down two plain white mugs from a shelf and fill them from a vacuum jug on the counter top.

He opened a bar fridge, taking out a carton of milk and placing it on the table in front of her. 'Sugar?'

Joanna shook her head. 'No, thanks—this smells wonderful.' She poured a dollop of milk into her coffee. McKellar, she noticed, took his black with no sugar.

'So—how can I help you, Mrs Winters? Or do you prefer Ms?' His eyes widened in polite query.

Joanna's mouth twitched. 'Actually, it's Doctor. But I'd much prefer Joanna.'

His expression gave nothing away. 'Joanna it is, then. And I prefer Matt. If I hear Matthew, I'm inclined to think my mother's on my case.'

Joanna gave a spontaneous chuckle. She had no wish to *mother* him. Far from it. And that wayward thought sent a flush to her cheeks. She hastily dragged her mind back to her surroundings and the reasons why she was here. 'About this calendar…'

'Is there a problem?' McKellar took a mouthful of his coffee.

Make it a thousand. Joanna's fingers curled around the handle of her mug like a lifeline. 'For starters, Jason is under age.'

The silence was deafening, and something about its quality made her bring her gaze up and look searchingly at the man opposite.

'He didn't tell me.' McKellar's voice was flat. 'On the other hand, I didn't ask.' He lifted a shoulder expressively. 'A stupid mistake on my part. I just assumed he was older. He's a big lad.'

'He's like his father.' Joanna's eyes softened. 'Damon played rugby for the state. He died before Jason was born—non-Hodgkin's lymphoma. He was twenty-one…'

There was an echo of deep silence, until Matt broke it very quietly. 'Life really chucks it at us sometimes, doesn't it?'

She nodded, embarrassed. It was the first time in a long time she'd felt the overwhelming need to mention those very early days. And why on earth now? she fretted. With this man? He'd begin to think she was some kind of nut case. To cover her confusion, she lifted her mug and took a gulp of coffee.

'I take you don't want Jason involved in the making of the calendar, then?' Matt gave her a sliding, sidelong glance, before swinging up out of his chair and going to the window, looking out. He half turned his head. 'It will be tastefully done with a professional photographer.'

'I'm sure...' Joanna bit the inside of her cheek. Was she being old-fashioned, over-protective, out of touch with present-day mores?

While she hesitated, Matt turned to face her, parking himself against the window-ledge, as if preparing to do battle. 'These days, there's nothing shocking about clubs of all descriptions opting to raise funds this way, you know. In fact, didn't I read the other day that a group of rural women in their quite senior years did a light-hearted shoot to raise money for a new stage curtain in their farmers' hall?'

'Well, you may have done.' Joanna lifted a shoulder. 'And I'm not shocked,' she added. 'I'm a doctor, for heaven's sake! But I would rather my son waits until he's a bit more emotionally mature before opting to take off his clothes for a calendar shoot.'

'Fair enough.' Matt reached for his coffee and drained it, clattering his mug back onto the bench top. 'And don't worry.' He met her eyes and she could see the faintest hint of amusement in their depths. 'Jason needn't know you've been here. I'll let him down lightly. He's a good kid.'

'Thanks.' Joanna got awkwardly to her feet. 'That's really all I came for and I'm probably keeping you from your work...'

'You're not,' he dismissed. In an abrupt movement, he moved towards the door, astounded by his train of thought. He didn't want her to leave. And how crazy was that? 'Would you like to see over the place?' Oh, hell! He winced silently. He must appear like an overeager puppy trying to impress. He saw her glance at her watch and cringed even further. 'Another time, perhaps. You probably need to get to your own work.'

'No...' She shook back her silky dark hair, a tentative smile edging her mouth. 'I have a few minutes and I'd like to see where Jason's been spending his leisure time.'

Matt gave her the grand tour, his manner suddenly upbeat, his expression mobile, as he gestured with well-shaped, long-fingered hands.

And Joanna was impressed, particularly with the thought that had been given to access for the disabled.

'We like to term it ''differently abled'',' Matt said.

How enlightened. 'Do you get many?'

'Only one or two yet. But I'm liasing with the hospital all the time, getting the news out there. We're happy to see anyone whose capability has been lost for any reason—not specifically sporting. Often we can get folk on an exercise programme to give them a much better quality of life.' He gave a controlled smile. 'And if we can save them sitting for hours in a rehab centre somewhere, waiting for their turn, so much the better.'

Joanna nodded. She was impressed beyond words. There was so much good work going to be happening here, much more than she'd imagined. 'Oh, you have indoor courts as well!'

Matt had wound back a set of folding doors to reveal not only the usual gym equipment but courts for both basketball and soccer, plus male and female changing rooms.

'At the moment we're concentrating on basketball.

Jason's in the junior team. Did he tell you?'

'Not specifically,' Joanna said honestly. 'He told me he's involved in lots of things here. Should he be paying a fee…?' The thought had just occurred to her. Obviously the place didn't run itself. 'He hasn't asked for extra money…'

Matt registered her look of vulnerability and hastened to reassure her. 'If they can afford it, the lads kick in a few dollars for the use of the place, maintenance and so on. That side of things is my baby.' His mouth twisted. 'I grew up in a country town where there was never enough happening for young people. And while Glenville isn't a country town, it's a smallish regional city for all that, with not a lot being offered towards teenage recreation.'

He was right, Joanna realised. Apart from what was organised for them at school, the kids had nothing much beside the movies and a ten-pin bowling alley to keep them off the streets. She supposed she should be grateful Matt McKellar had taken up the challenge and done something about it. She smiled a bit uncertainly. 'But the sports medicine side of things is your real business, isn't it?'

'Absolutely.' He jammed his hands into his back pockets as they continued to make their way through the precincts. 'My background is in orthopaedics but I'm happy to speak to anyone who has concerns about their level of fitness.

'Whether it's losing weight or putting on weight, they need to know how to go about it initially. And because we're specialised, we can supply the answers more comprehensively than perhaps their GP could.

Nothing against general practitioners,' he said with a laugh, raising both hands as if to ward off her expected critical response.

'And before you begin to imagine I'm filthy rich,' he continued, 'I haven't done any of this on my own. I may have had the idea originally, but the place is owned and run by a consortium. We have accredited coaches, a couple of physios on staff—in fact, here's one of them now. Morning, Elle.'

'Matt.' A tall, leggy blonde clad in white shorts and T-shirt sent him a wide white smile before disappearing through a set of swing doors to what was presumably a staffroom.

'She seems very young.' How absurd to feel a twist of resentment! It was none of her business who Matt McKellar chose to work with him.

'But very capable.' Following Joanna's gaze after the young physio, Matt added carefully, 'And in case you're concerned, we're fully insured against accidents.' He finally completed the tour and walked her back to the entrance. 'Everyone who joins the club receives a leaflet on its philosophies and workings. Jason should have had one.'

Joanna gave a hollow laugh. 'It's probably still at the bottom of his sports bag.'

His mouth twitched into a grin and Joanna found he was holding the door open for her in a display of old-fashioned courtesy.

In a second the atmosphere between them was charged with awareness. Joanna felt her mouth dry. What on earth was going on here? She took a step, hovering in the doorway, as if something beyond her control was delaying her, keeping her within

McKellar's orbit. She swallowed a bit unevenly. 'Thanks, again, Dr McKellar—Matt.'

'My pleasure.'

Joanna adjusted her bag, her fingers biting into the soft leather of her shoulder strap. 'I, uh, feel very reassured now about Jason spending time here.'

Another awkward silence descended over them and Matt broke it, fixing her with a sudden searing blue look. 'You should be very proud of your son, Joanna. He needn't have told you anything about the calendar but he obviously respected the values you've instilled in him. Take care.' He raised a hand in a farewell salute and closed the door.

Matt stepped back into the foyer, lifting his hands to bracket his head. Hell's bells. He took a hard indrawn breath and let it go, and then on impulse he turned, sprinting back up to his office, taking the stairs two at a time. Inside, he was drawn to the window like a thirsting animal to a running stream.

He looked down just in time to see Joanna Winters emerge from the walkway and begin making her way across the car park to stop beside a dark blue nifty little sports car.

Watching her, he felt as though an invisible punch had landed in his solar plexus, robbing him not just of oxygen but of reason as well. And he was only too aware of another tightness elsewhere, an awareness, a longing that had lain dormant for longer than he cared to remember. Too long...

He shook his head. She *was* lovely. There was a sweet vulnerability about her that was already threatening to drag out the male protectiveness in him. Was he ready for that to happen? He yanked himself up short and with a barely discernible shake of his head turned away from the window.

Hell, after all this time he wouldn't even know the rules.

Joanna drove towards the Strachan medical practice, her reflexes almost automatic. Slowing for the red traffic light, she studied her hands lying loosely on the steering-wheel. If she hadn't known better, she'd have said they looked relaxed.

How deceptive appearances could be.

She took a deep breath, swinging round a traffic island to join the line of cars heading over the bridge to the northern side of the city.

'Damn,' she murmured quite mildly, easing her car into her usual parking bay at the clinic. She had a full day ahead of her. But how on earth was she going to concentrate? Letting her head go back on the seat for just a second, she closed her eyes and could see Matt McKellar's magnetic blue eyes, hear the rich huskiness of his voice. She tried his name in her head. Matt. Nice, uncomplicated.

And tell that to the marines, she huffed silently, opening the door and swinging out of the car. Unless she'd completely lost her feminine intuition, there was nothing uncomplicated about McKellar. Stifling a sigh, she retrieved her case from the boot of the car and made her way across to the low-set brick building.

'Oh, don't you look terrific!' Steffi Phillips, the practice receptionist, arched an eyebrow. 'Lunch date?'

'Nice thought.' Joanna's mouth tipped into a wry smile. 'What do you have for me, Stef?'

'You're booked solid.' Steffi lowered her voice to

add, 'And Moya Kirkland's been here since nine o'clock. She's listed for an excision at ten. A bit up-tight, poor pet.'

Joanna glanced at her watch. It was fifteen minutes to the hour. 'Well, let's not keep her fretting.' She took the pile of patient cards Steffi had ready for her. 'Show Mrs Kirkland into the small treatment room, please, Stef. I'll buzz Kate to get her prepped.'

A few minutes later, Joanna made her way along the tiled corridor to the treatment room. It was hardly high-powered medicine she practised these days, she reflected and wondered whether after almost six years in general practice, she was subconsciously looking for a change.

Forget it, Joanna, she chided inwardly. With a teen-ager who outgrew his clothes almost weekly and who ate as much as two grown men, she needed a regular income. This was no time to start being picky about her career.

Pushing aside the cheerful peach and gold-patterned curtain, she greeted her elderly patient. 'Good morning, Moya. All ready for your little op?'

'I do hope so, Doctor.' The anxiety in Moya's eyes moderated slightly at Joanna's warm manner.

'You'll be fine.' Joanna double-checked the notes. Moya's blood pressure was normal and, apart from the recurring problem relating to sun-damaged skin on her face and the backs of her hands, she enjoyed reasonably good health. Today, though, Moya looked unusually small and vulnerable, her neat black shoes placed side by side under the chair at the foot of the treatment couch, her large shopping bag placed on the chair itself.

Joanna stroked back the elderly woman's hair gently, revealing a red, scaly patch running parallel with the lower end of her eyebrow at the temple. 'We've treated this twice with freezing, Moya,' she commented. 'But it's a stubborn one. I'll excise it for you today. That should stop it in its tracks.'

Moya's pale eyes fluttered briefly. 'I trust you to do the right thing by me, dear.'

Taking Moya's hand, Joanna exchanged a smile with Kate, the practice nurse. 'Are we right to go?'

Kate nodded, indicating the small trolley she'd set out ready for the procedure.

'Now, Moya, I'm just going to wash my hands and then we'll start off by giving you a local anaesthetic,' Joanna explained gently. 'It'll make the side of your face quite numb so you won't feel any discomfort when I operate.'

She heard the old lady's long sigh before she closed her eyes.

Gowned and gloved, Joanna expertly drew up the lignocaine. 'This will pack quite a sting, Moya,' she warned, and began slowly infiltrating the area. Stoic little pet, she thought, disposing of the needle into a sharps container. 'We'll need to wait a little while and then I'll whip off this nasty little number and stitch you back nice and neatly.'

'Could I still go along to my bingo, Dr Winters? I always go on a Wednesday. It's on at St James's church hall.'

'If you're feeling OK when we've finished, I don't see any reason why not,' Joanna said. 'Perhaps we could arrange a taxi for you down to the hall.'

Moya clicked her tongue. 'I don't need a taxi, dear.

It's only half a block away. Besides,' she added, a serene little smile curving her mouth, 'my friend Edward's outside, waiting for me. We'll walk along together. There'll be a nice cuppa tea when we get there.' Her brow puckered fleetingly. 'I won't look a fright, will I?'

'No, Moya, you won't.' Joanna stifled a chuckle, winking at Kate as she adjusted the sterile drape. 'Your hair will camouflage most of it anyway.'

Satisfied the area around the lesion was now quite numb, Joanna picked up a scalpel and began to work swiftly, relieved when she got the entire scaly top section off almost complete. It looked quite inoffensive lying on the plastic slide, but only expert analysis would reaffirm that it was so.

And with Queensland having one of the highest rates of sun cancers in the world, health professionals had to be ever-vigilant when patients presented with even the merest trace of skin damage.

Twenty minutes later Joanna had finished. 'There you are, Moya, all done.'

'Fancy!' her elderly patient said in some amazement. 'I didn't feel a thing.'

Joanna chuckled. 'I should hope not. This dressing will need to be replaced each day, Moya. It's only a patch and quite easy to remove if you soften the edges with warm salty water. Try not to get the actual wound area wet, though. Just ask for Cutiplast at the chemist. They'll be able to fix you up with a supply. Would you like me to jot all that down for you?'

Moya looked relieved. 'That might be helpful, thank you, Doctor.'

'Right, I'll do that now, while Kate's clearing

away,' Joanna said kindly. 'Then pop back in a week and I'll remove the stitches and we'll have a chat about the lab result.'

'I'm most grateful for all the care you've taken.'

'You're welcome, Moya.' Tugging off her gown, Joanna aimed it at the bin. Another satisfied customer. She went out into the corridor. Perhaps general practice did have its moments after all.

Walking past Reception to her own consulting room, she was deep in thought. Steffi had to hail her twice before she registered. 'Call for you.' The receptionist held the receiver aloft, her hand over the mouthpiece. 'Dr McKellar.'

Joanna stopped short, the speed with which he'd moved sending her heart fluttering in alarm. A wave of sheer panic hollowed out her insides, yet her body began to sing, more alive than it had been for an age.

'Ah...' She clamped her bottom lip. 'Switch it through, please, Stef. I'll take it in my office.'

CHAPTER TWO

JOANNA moved across to her desk, the blinking light on the phone telling her the call had been connected. Taking a deep, calming breath, she picked up the receiver and said crisply, 'Joanna Winters.'

'Hi, Joanna. It's Matt McKellar.'

His voice startled her, its deep tones raising goosebumps all over her arms. 'Matt—hello.'

'Hello, yourself.'

The tension suddenly left her in a laughing question. 'Did I forget something?'

'No—but I did. I meant to invite you to a barbecue on Saturday week. Might be a good chance for you to link up with some of the people associated with the centre and with the other parents as well. That's if you're free, of course.'

Joanna heard the almost boyish eagerness in his voice and melted inside. 'Yes, I should be. Thanks. It sounds fun. Where and what time?'

'We're just finalising the arrangements. I'll let you know the details via Jason. OK?'

'Fine.' She found she was holding the receiver like a lifeline. 'Thanks again.'

Matt put the phone down, refusing to give house room to the mocking voice that questioned his motives in manufacturing a reason to contact Joanna Winters so quickly. He scrubbed lean fingers across his cheeks, feeling his stomach turn upside down. He hadn't been able to help himself. Perhaps it would turn out to be no more than a one-sided physical attraction. Whatever, he seemed compelled to find out.

Picking up the phone once more, he punched out his sister's number. It wasn't much notice but Deb would come through for him, he was sure...

'The guys for your quit-smoking group are all assembled.' Elle popped her head round the door. 'I've given them their name-tags.'

'Thanks. I'll be right there.' Matt clicked the phone back on its rest. No answer. He'd catch Deb later. 'Oh, Elle?' He swung off his chair. 'I'm arranging a barbecue for staff and parents of the junior lads' basketball team for Saturday week. Could you run off some flyers, please?' He sent her a hopeful, crooked grin. 'Same details as we had for last month's. It'll be at my sister's again.'

Elle rolled her eyes. 'It's time we got some permanent office help around here, Matthew.'

'Leave it with me.' He shot out of his office and began sprinting down the stairs towards one of the small conference rooms.

Elle looked narrowly after him. Now what's got the usually reserved Dr McKellar all fired up and perky this morning? she wondered.

Five professional sports people had shown up for Matt's clinic. His eyes lit with enthusiasm. 'Congratulations, people. You've taken the first step towards chucking your addiction to tobacco.'

'Not a good look for a sports jock, is it, Doc?' Chris Kinnane, a young fair-haired member of the senior basketball team, sat back in his chair, arms folded across his chest. 'The young kids look up to us. I feel guilty every time I light up.'

There was a general murmur of agreement around the table.

'My husband and I want to try for a baby next year.' Melissa Jackson, the only female in the group, was already looking discouraged. 'This is my third attempt to give up.'

'I'd be happy if I could just cut down,' Ben Arthur, a well-known long-distance runner, said ruefully.

'Cutting down is good,' Matt said carefully. 'But stopping should be your goal. And don't be fooled into thinking smoking lower-strength cigarettes will make a difference. It won't—you'll just inhale harder.'

There were discreet groans from several of the assembly.

'So, where do we start, Doc?'

Matt looked around the group with an air of optimism. He loved this part of his job, the teaching part. It was affirming, positive and so rewarding when your patients felt empowered enough to make this great change towards a healthier lifestyle.

'You're all here because you want to quit smoking,' he said. 'So, for the moment, let's just concentrate on the positives. And remember there aren't any miracles. The power to quit has to come from within yourselves.'

'I smoke around twenty a day,' Melissa confessed almost defiantly, pleating a strand of pale blonde hair behind her ear. 'If I gave up properly, how soon would I notice a difference in my health?'

'Quite quickly.' Matt turned his head towards her.

'After only six hours your heart rate and blood pressure begin decreasing. After twenty-four hours the carbon monoxide is out of your system. Your lungs are already beginning to function more efficiently. After three months, and this is good news for you especially, Mel, there's a definite increase in your fertility.'

'Oh.' Melissa blushed. 'That quickly?'

Matt nodded. 'And better still, and this goes for all of you, after five years your risk of a heart attack is almost the same as for a non-smoker.'

There was a ripple of optimism around the oval table. A new sense of purpose amongst the group.

'Bring on the old will-power, then, eh, Doc?' Chris twitched his mouth into a rueful grin.

'The same way you use it to excel in your chosen sports. If you want it enough...' Matt palmed his hands and then brought them together in a unifying gesture '...you'll do it. Today, I'm going to give each of you a calendar. I want you to make a decision now and write down the date you will quit smoking.'

''Struth.' Ben Arthur chewed his bottom lip. 'I don't know if I can do that, Doc.'

'All I'm asking you to do, Ben, is to set yourself a quit day,' Matt stated calmly. 'After that, I'll speak to each of you individually and we'll do some preparation that hopefully will give you your best chance of success. Remember, we're here to support you, not judge you.'

'In that case, then...' Ben began poring over the calendar Matt placed in front of him.

Joanna dropped with a sigh onto the big old-fashioned sofa in her lounge room, eased off her shoes and tucked her feet under her bottom. Friday evening at last. Two days since she'd met Matt McKellar.

Reaching across to the side table, she picked up the glass of wine she'd poured earlier. She took a mouthful, letting the cool sweetness linger in her mouth for a second before she swallowed it.

Matt.

She snuggled deeper into the sofa, remembering his smile, fleeting, almost gone before it was properly there. Her mouth folded into a soft contemplative moue. Perhaps he was merely out of practice. But why? And, more to the point, why on earth were her thoughts so occupied with the man? Why were her hormones singing, snapping to attention as if she were sixteen again, for heaven's sake!

'Jason?' She turned her head, wincing as the front door was flung open and banged shut. 'I'm in here.'

Bounding into the room, her son skidded to a stop. 'Hi.' He flopped onto the other end of the sofa. 'What's to eat?'

They exchanged mother-to-son grins. 'Dinner in fifteen minutes. Can you wait that long?'

'I guess.'

'How was training?'

'Good,' the boy said economically. 'And you'll be pleased to know I'm not in the calendar shoot.'

'Oh?' Joanna felt her heart pick up its rhythm. On one hand, she felt elated Matt had come through for her, but on the other she'd have had to be made of rock not to sense her son's disappointment.

'We're not doing it at all.' Jason hooked one leg over the arm of the settee. 'Matt's lined up a couple of corporate sponsors to pay for the new abseiling gear and he said we'll run a mega-raffle to raise the bucks for the canteen.'

Joanna sat forward and swung her feet to the floor. Heavens! She hadn't meant McKellar to go that far!

Jason reached into the pocket of his track jacket. 'I've a flyer for you from Matt. Invitation to a barbecue and stuff for parents on Saturday week. It's all here.' He passed over the slightly crumpled sheet of yellow paper.

'Oh. OK. I suppose I should make an effort and go, then?' Joanna dredged up a smile, groping for normality.

'Whatever.' Jason jackknifed from the sofa. 'I'll hit the shower before dinner.'

'Mmm,' Joanna said absently, and began smoothing out the flyer.

As they sat down to their meal, Joanna said casually, 'This barbecue is being held at Featherdale. Isn't that out of town a bit?'

'A few Ks.' Jason dug into his jacket potato with youthful appetite. 'It's a farm. We went there on a field trip from school this year. They have quolls in captivity.'

'Quolls?' Joanna sent him a questioning look. 'Those little marsupials that look like cats? I don't think I've ever seen one.'

'You probably haven't. They're a threatened species,' the boy enlightened her. 'We learnt about them as part of our science project.'

Joanna forked a path through her peas. 'So, does M— Dr McKellar live at Featherdale or what?'

Jason lifted a shoulder. 'Don't think so. He's got a flat in town somewhere.'

Oh, well, she could ask around at the surgery, Joanna decided. Someone was bound to know something.

An early phone call at work on Monday solved her dilemma.

Joanna had been at the window in her consulting room, staring out. For the whole of the weekend she'd felt unsettled, dreamy. Dreamy? She snorted. That emotion was for teenagers. Get a grip, she told herself impatiently, turning with a sigh when her phone rang.

'Dr McKellar for you again.' Steffi's tone had a knowing, sing-song quality about it.

'Put him through, please.' In return, Joanna's manner was crisp. But her heartbeat had the fluttering quality of a trapped bird.

'Not crowding you, am I?' Matt asked when Joanna came on the line.

'Of course not,' she told him quickly, picturing him, remembering his mannerism of pushing his fingers back through his hair. Was he doing that now? she wondered. The thought warmed her, distracted her. 'What can I do for you?'

'It's more what I can do for you—that's if you'll allow me.'

Curiouser and curiouser. Joanna lowered herself onto the edge of her desk.

'I, uh, wondered if I might offer you a lift out to Featherdale on Saturday.'

'That's nice of you,' she said after a moment, surprised at how steady her voice sounded.

'It'll be dark early so I'll collect you about five.

That'll give me time to show you around before the fun starts, OK?'

Joanna's fingers went to the silver chain at her throat and grasped the tiny medallion. 'Fine. Do you have my address?'

'It'll be on Jason's registration,' Matt confirmed. He didn't add he'd memorised it already. 'Till Saturday, then. Goodbye, Joanna.'

Matt clipped the receiver back on its rest. He'd done it! He sat back down in his chair with a motion more like falling. Closing his eyes, he let his thoughts run riot.

Joanna got through the week in a haze of unreality. By Friday afternoon, she was almost giddy with anticipation.

Showing her patient out of the treatment room, she turned back, impatient with her wayward thoughts. Tugging off the light cotton gown, she washed her hands with undue vigour. Even that distraction didn't help.

Still she thought of Matt McKellar.

But if anything did happen between them, it would be complex, she acknowledged. There was Jason for a start...

She made a sound of frustration. Wasn't she jumping the gun just a tad? Returning to her consulting room, she picked up the card from her desk and went out to the waiting room to call her last patient for the day.

Sharon Nolan was a new patient. Joanna glanced at the card, noting her date of birth placed the young woman at eighteen years of age. 'So, Sharon.' She smiled. 'What can I do for you today?'

'It's all a bit embarrassing.' The young woman grimaced, her even white teeth edging nervously along her lower lip. 'I've got this tattoo…'

Joanna leaned forward attentively. 'Has it become a problem?'

'Kind of.' Sharon shook back her ash-blonde hair, which shimmied past her shoulders. 'It's my boyfriend, Rhys…'

Joanna held back a smile. 'He doesn't like it?'

'He doesn't know about it.' Soft heat brushed Sharon's cheeks and she swallowed. 'It's…on my rump.'

Joanna lifted an eyebrow. She could see where the young woman was headed. 'Is it unsightly? Is that the problem?'

'It's awful! Well, I suppose it's not that awful,' she reconsidered. 'But I got it done when I was sixteen— Mum didn't know. But my boyfriend then was called Aaron so I got two hearts tattooed with our names…' She looked appealingly at Joanna and they both laughed—Sharon a bit reluctantly, it had to be admitted.

Joanna picked up her pen, tapping it end to end on her desk. 'So you'd like the tattoo removed, is that it?'

Sharon pulled a face. 'Would it hurt a lot?'

'Probably not half as much as getting it on in the first place,' Joanna said bluntly. 'I can refer you to a cosmetic surgeon specialising in the removal of tattoos, but you'd have to go to Brisbane. Would that be a problem?'

Sharon shook her head. 'I attend uni there anyway. I'm only home in Glenville for a swot vac.' She bit her lip. 'I won't be left with tell-tale ugly marks, will I?'

'I wouldn't think so.' Joanna was reassuring. 'Skin is pretty amazing stuff. The doctor would most likely use a tissue expander. The idea of this is to increase the area of skin available so that when your tattoo is removed, the wound can be covered by your own skin. It should all heal nicely, perhaps with only a very fine scar line.'

Sharon blinked. 'I've heard about laser treatment,' she said tentatively.

'Well, that's a possibility as well.' Joanna flicked open her referral pad. 'Just be aware that everyone's biology is different so not everyone is a suitable candidate for laser treatment.' She looked up and smiled. 'But as you seem keen, I'll give you a note for Charles Hunter. He's a dermatologist at our local hospital. In fact, it's probably the best place for you to start. And if, when he examines you, he's of the opinion you'd be better off with a cosmetic surgeon, he'll refer you on.'

'Thanks, Doctor.' Sharon's rather beautiful green eyes lit up. 'That's brilliant.' She turned up the collar on her little fake-fur jacket. 'I promise I won't ever do anything mad like that again.'

'What do you think of tattoos?' Joanna directed the question light-heartedly to her son. It was the next morning and they were in the kitchen, washing up from their weekly Saturday treat of a cooked breakfast.

'Why? Are you thinking of getting one?' Jason grinned, dodging the spray of detergent bubbles she flicked at him. 'Some of them are cool.' He shrugged. 'Some are gross.'

'Well, if ever you're tempted to get one...' Joanna rinsed a plate and placed it in the drainer '...talk to me first, please, love.'

'No worries, Jo-Jo,' Jason responded cheekily. He swivelled a glance at the little carriage clock on top of the fridge. 'I'd better take off for work.'

'Want me to run you?'

'Nah. I'll take the bike.'

'I'm going to this barbecue tonight, don't forget.' Joanna lifted a soapy hand to brush back a strand of hair from her cheek. 'Do you want to ask Daniel over, get a pizza?'

Jason shifted a bit awkwardly. 'Uh, we thought we'd catch an early movie and then go on for a burger. We're meeting Skye and Amber.' He dropped his gaze. 'It's not a date or anything...'

Joanna covered her faint surprise with a smile. 'Do you need extra money?'

'No, thanks.' He aimed a thump at the louvre door as he turned to go through. 'Got paid this week.'

Of course it was a date. Joanna was thoughtful as she wiped down the counter top with a long sweep of her sponge. She shouldn't be surprised. Her son was in his seventeenth year. Girls would have to be high on his agenda.

Sighing, she shook out a fresh teatowel and began to dry the dishes. If Damon had lived, they would have shared their son's growing pains, leant on one another for parenting support. Well, it wasn't going to happen. Not ever.

Throughout the day, indecision was coiling a knot in her stomach. Should she tell Jason that Matt was calling for her—or not?

We've hardly met! she protested silently to the winter roses, stripping the spent blooms before picking a bunch of the splashy yellows and reds for the vases. It might all fizzle out, she rationalised, and it's not like a date or anything… Her son's words came back to unsettle her all over again.

She was being ridiculously coy. Joanna gave herself a mental shake. Of course her son needed to know her arrangements for the evening. And she'd tell him the moment he arrived home from his Saturday job.

In the end it proved almost a non-event.

'Matt's probably giving some of the others a lift as well.' Jason gave her a look much older than his years. 'He drives the club's mini-bus all over the place.'

Joanna's spirits dropped like a stone. How naïve she'd been to assume Matt's offer of transport had been anything more than just that. Reality settled like oil on the sparkling waters of her expectations. She bit her lips together. You've been indulging in pipedreams, she berated herself, turning away with a little twitch of her shoulder.

When it was time to get ready, she hardly knew what she put on—or cared, she qualified thinly, pulling on jeans and a plain silk shirt. Nevertheless, she brushed her hair until it shone, took care with her make-up and was reasonably pleased with her appearance when her front doorbell rang.

Assuming it was Matt, she hastily slipped on a short, biker-style jacket and went to let him in.

'Hello…' She blinked out into the soft light, reacquainting herself with the shape of him, trying not to stare but noting he was casually dressed in jeans and a white crew-neck jumper that accentuated his lean darkness.

His eyes flinted briefly. 'Not too early, am I?'

'No.' Her breath lodged in her throat and she motioned him inside. 'I'm quite ready. I…um…just have to locate my mobile. Won't be a tick.'

Matt let out a steadying breath, jamming his hands into his back pockets and looking around the slightly cluttered living room. She's a natural home-maker, he decided and wondered why the idea pleased him.

His gaze sharpened, lingering on the cluster of photographs and then dropping to the richly coloured rugs that gave the room a welcoming warmth. Slowly his gaze circled the room and dwelt with a longing he couldn't explain on the old-fashioned sofa that faced the open fireplace…

In a second his musing was interrupted and he spun round, hearing what he presumed was the soft closing of her bedroom door. And then she was there in the room with him. He caught the waft of her perfume, subtle, teasing his senses. 'All set?'

'Finally.' She flushed and laughed uncertainly. 'Should I bring my bag?'

'Not unless you particularly want to. I'm well equipped for emergencies.'

They stepped out into the porch and Matt turned to pull the front door closed, the action causing his hand to brush Joanna's shoulder. She took a sharp little breath, a feeling of awareness putting her off balance, leaving a tingling sensation in its wake.

Feeling a sense of unreality that he was here with her, that this evening had happened at all, she turned her gaze sharply towards the street, expecting to see the parked bulk of a mini-bus. She blinked uncertainly. There was no such vehicle in sight. Instead, a discreet, silver-grey Mercedes was hugging the kerb.

Joanna suddenly wanted to laugh, to dance.

'What?'

She saw Matt's dark brows flex in query and let the happiness bubble out. 'You came in a car!'

'You expected a motorbike? Dammit!' His head went back and he slammed one fist against the open palm of his other hand. 'I knew I'd get it wrong.'

Joanna gave a snip of laughter, deciding to play along with the silly game. 'Can't blame a girl for hoping.'

'Or a guy, for that matter...'

Joanna's heart crashed against her ribs. His voice had dropped, gone all husky, creeping right over her bones. Her perceptions were suddenly heightened, becoming as taut as a trip-wire. And he was close, so close she had to tilt her head to look at him.

And when their eyes met, the impact was searing, as if they were being drawn inexorably to where the outcome was already preordained.

Joanna felt her safe world tilt and emotions she'd thought buried began stirring, clamouring for light, for the chance to grow and blossom. She swallowed the sudden dryness in her throat as her body responded to his nearness, his maleness...

Somewhere in the back of her mind she registered

his slow movement. And then she was in his arms, as though they were about to dance. So close she could feel the strength and line of his lean body.

She shivered at the strangeness, yet at the same time recognised the familiarity of once more being in a man's embrace.

Matt tightened his arms about her, the shock of contact with her female softness shattering him to the core, as though some tight screw had suddenly unwound and set him free. On a strangled breath, he bent to her, placing the softest kiss on each eyelid before brushing her mouth once, twice, three times.

Joanna's eyes flickered open, the whispered touch of his lips leaving fire shimmering all over her skin. Her breath fluttered out in a long sigh and, drawing back slowly, she lifted weighted lids to stare bemusedly into his eyes. She swallowed. 'That was a bit unexpected, wasn't it?'

Opalescent fire shone in his blue eyes. 'I feel as though I've been hung up by my heels.'

A ghost of a smile touched her mouth and she placed her hands against the solidity of his chest. 'That doesn't sound very safe.'

'Do you want to be *safe*, Joanna?' His tone was burred with sensual awareness and he sought her lips again.

Opening her mouth to his, Joanna kissed him back, her body, with a mind of its own, stretching slinkily against his. She caught him closer, locking her hands at the back of his head, and for a few seconds it was as though they were in the grip of a flood-tide that was sweeping them out to a dark sea of sheer sensation.

Then just as suddenly it was over. Like a fever that had passed.

'Oh.' Joanna exhaled a ragged little breath and buried her face in his chest, breathing in the warm male closeness of him like lifesaving oxygen.

After a while Matt put her gently from him and then drew her back as if he couldn't help himself. His chest lifted in a long sigh. 'I guess we should make tracks,' he murmured into the softness of her hair.

'Guess so…'

CHAPTER THREE

MATT was silent as they drove, and several times Joanna glanced at his still profile, before she asked, 'So, why Featherdale?'

'Ah…' He seemed to gather himself. 'It's my sister Debra's place. She and her husband, Scott, are attached to the Parks and Wildlife Department. They have interested groups through the place all the time and the facilities to cater for them. Which suits me.' He sent her a fleeting grin. 'Socially, it takes a hell of a lot off my shoulders and I'd rather see them get the club's business than anyone else.'

'That makes sense.' Joanna leaned back on the soft leather. 'Jason said his class had been out to Featherdale on a science field trip recently.'

'Deb and Scott do quite a bit of research,' Matt confirmed. 'They're both science graduates but there was no way they wanted to be stuck in a lab all day so this is the answer they came up with.'

'It sounds fascinating.' Joanna smiled, cocooned in a bubble of wildly mixed emotions she wasn't about to explore.

'Do you like being a GP?'

'For the most part, yes.' At the abrupt change of conversation, Joanna tried to capture her thoughts, which were spinning, fracturing like ice under heat.

'And I have to earn a living,' she pointed out on a jagged laugh.

'Yes, I imagine you do.' Matt's rejoinder was bland.

Featherdale was a low, sprawling farmhouse, its front verandah heavily laced with greenery. In the distance, Joanna could see a windmill, its blades silent now in the still air of early evening.

'Two hectares at the back are under vines,' Matt told her, as they bumped gently along the track and drew to a stop at the rear of the house.

'I'd no idea there were any vineyards in the district.'

'See, you've learned something already.' He curved her a brief smile. 'Deb and Scott make a rather nice Shiraz. You'll probably get to sample it this evening.'

As they got out of the car, a black streak flew towards Matt in an explosion of joyful tail-wagging.

'Hello, boy!' He was clearly in thrall, bending over the dog's wide, blunt features, rubbing him between the ears. 'This is Finchly.' He grinned.

Joanna looked on delightedly. 'He's a Staffy.' She recognised the terrier breed. 'They're very people-friendly, aren't they?'

'Mmm.' Matt's rubbing tapered off. 'Great with kids.' He moved to unlatch the back gate.

'Do your sister and her husband have children?'

'Twin boys, Andrew and Hamish. They're eleven. And talk of the little devils…' Turning his head, he shaded his eyes and looked down the track a bit to where the youngsters had appeared from under the drooping foliage of a bottlebrush. They were toting small fishing rods.

'Hey, Uncle Matt!' the childish voices called in unison.

'Hey, guys!' Matt beckoned with his arm. 'Come and meet Joanna.'

'They're like two peas in a pod,' Joanna said, laughing, after the introductions had been made and the sandy-haired duo had run off about their own business.

'Hamish has more freckles.' Matt chuckled. 'They're great kids...'

Joanna looked sharply at him, surprising a look of yearning in his eyes before the shutters came down and he spoke with forced cheerfulness: 'Let's find Deb, shall we? She's probably in the kitchen.'

They went through a vine-covered pergola and up the back steps. Joanna caught the aroma of spices and baking as Matt pushed open the door of the big farmhouse kitchen.

'Hi, big brother!' Debra Carlisle turned from rescuing something from the oven. 'Come on in.' Sliding the baking tray onto the bench top, she drew off her oven mitt and came forward to hug her sibling.

'This is Joanna Winters, Deb.' Matt made the introductions, keeping his hand loosely on his sister's shoulder.

Debra's eyes widened fractionally. 'Joanna.' She smiled, offering her hand. 'Welcome to Featherdale.'

'Thank you. Matt's told me lots about it already.'

'And I promised Joanna a glass of your Shiraz,' Matt said with a lazy smile.

'Oh, I'm sure that can be arranged.' Debra batted him playfully with her oven mitt. 'But for now, be a love and go see what you can do for Scott, would you, please? For some reason he's way behind schedule. He'll be screaming for help any second.'

'I'm on my way.' Matt leaned across the bench and tore off a wedge from the freshly baked herb bread. 'Just to keep me going,' he said with a grin, slamming the screen door as he left.

'He's happy.' Debra's thoughtful comment came after a longish pause. 'Anything to do with you, Joanna?' The laughing lilt in her voice took away any suggestion she was being nosy.

'We haven't known each other long.' Joanna flushed slightly. 'We actually met through my son, Jason. He's one of Matt's basketball hopefuls.'

'Oh, my gosh!' Debra picked up a sprig of rosemary and stripped it. 'You must have been a child bride!'

'I was eighteen.' Joanna laughed and then sobered. 'My husband died shortly after we were married.'

'Oh, how awful! What was it, an accident?'

'A form of cancer.' Almost defensively, Joanna flipped a teatowel from its rack and began to dry some plates that were in the drainer. Her expression closed. What was it about these McKellar siblings that seemed to draw out her innermost thoughts so easily?

'That is so sad, Joanna.' Debra got down a wooden bowl and began to tear greens for a salad. She shook her head. 'Both you and Matt must have drawn the short straw—' She stopped short, spinning round as the twins hurled themselves through the back door. 'Right, into the shower, you two. And did you get rid of that smelly bait?'

'Yes, Mum...' they chorused.

'Are we allowed to come to the barbecue?' Andrew asked.

'To eat only.' Their mother was firm.

Hamish sent a pleading smile to his mother. 'Dad said there'd be a camp fire so we could make real *billy* tea.'

Debra wavered. 'Well, maybe you can stick around for that, but afterwards you skedaddle, OK?'

'Yes!' The youngsters touched hands in a high-five salute and took off up the hallway.

Joanna chuckled. 'They're gorgeous, Deb.'

'Double trouble, more like it,' she countered with a wry grin. 'But so worth it.' She moved across to the sink to give her hands a quick rinse. 'Now, let's get that drink Matt promised you, shall we?'

'How many are you expecting?' Drink in hand, Joanna watched Deb sprinkle sultanas into a pan of rice and fold them through the savoury mixture.

'Oh—about twenty, I think. Just a few from Matt's staff and the rest are parents like yourself.'

'I really envy you.' Joanna shook her head, taking stock of the feast that was rapidly coming to fruition around them. 'You seem to do everything so naturally.' Her mouth turned down at the corners. 'I'm a pretty basic cook.'

'It's just practice,' Deb countered airily. 'And actually I enjoy preparing food, which is the crux of it, according to the experts.'

'Scott's about ready for the steaks, Deb.' Matt swung through the screen door, helping himself to a crisp radish from the salad bowl.

'In the fridge.' Debra hooked a tray out from a

recessed shelf. 'And there's some marinated chicken pieces to go as well. We'll chargrill those.'

'I'll take the salad, shall I?' Joanna put down her glass and picked up the huge wooden bowl.

'Lovely. Thanks, Joanna. Now, go and enjoy yourselves.' Debra shooed them off. 'The boys can manage the rest of the stuff.' She grinned. 'Their legs are much younger than ours after all.'

It was just after ten o'clock when Matt dropped into a canvas chair beside Joanna. 'You're looking very pensive,' he remarked, his teeth glinting in a smile that did odd things to her stomach.

Joanna swallowed the last of her tea, relishing the distinctive smoky taste from the logs of eucalypts used in the camp fire. 'I was just wondering if I'd mingled enough.'

'I'm sure you have.' He was firm. 'And thanks for all your help this evening.'

She turned her head slightly and looked at him. 'I enjoyed myself.'

'Hey, it's not over yet.' His eyes locked with hers and for an endless moment they stared at each other, then he abruptly turned away and drank from his own tea mug, and Joanna found she could breathe again.

'It's…all been lovely.' She made the comment almost to herself, leaning back into her chair, breathing in the crisp night air. The garden flares were sending out interesting shadows across the lawn and overhead a necklace of stars looked close enough to touch. Matt was close enough to touch as well… She bit her lip, feeling the tingle all the way up her arm. At the same moment, her gaze went to her hands, noticing the way they'd crept together in her lap without her even feeling it.

'Are you on a curfew this evening?'

She heard the smile in Matt's voice and looked sharply at him. 'Not really. Jason's well able to look after himself. Why do you ask?'

He lifted a shoulder. 'Someone's brought a guitar. Scott thought he'd build up the fire a bit and we could have a sing-song.'

'Sounds like fun.'

His mouth quirked into a wry smile. 'Not too homespun for you?'

She sent him a pained look.

'Come on, then, Doctor.' Matt jackknifed to his feet and held his hand out to her.

Joanna gave a breathy little laugh, leaning into him as he levered her upright.

'This seems to be going to waste.' Matt scooped up a woollen picnic rug someone had draped over the back of a chair. 'I'm sure we could make much better use of it.'

Joanna took a shallow breath, her heart tripping, as they began making their way across to the camp fire. It was as though she'd stepped into a dream sequence. And she wondered about this attraction between her and Matt McKellar. It had come out of nowhere. Would it disappear just as quickly? Doubts and questions as elusive as a butterfly's wing ran through her mind.

'Over here, I think.' Matt broke into her thoughts, leading her across to a little knoll where they were just slightly apart from the company but from where they had a magical view of the night-time shapes of the trees against the glow of the campfire.

When they were settled on the rug, he reached out and took her hand, linking their fingers. The atmosphere around them began to throb with the soft strumming of a guitar. And in another part of the garden an owl purred deep in its throat.

Joanna felt a long shiver of awareness and turned her head towards him, but in the semi-darkness it was difficult to see more than the outline of his face. But she sensed she could feel him breathing, feel the beat of his pulse under her thumb as it curled against his wrist.

Matt tightened his grip on her fingers, feeling her respond. He wanted to draw her closer, much closer, bury his face in her hair, breathe in her perfume. His throat worked as he swallowed. 'Joanna...'

Suddenly their absorption with one another was shattered as starkly as the crack of a rifle in an arctic wilderness.

A piercing cry of anguish had come from Scott. Moving without his usual care and attention to stoke up the camp fire, he'd tripped and fallen headlong into the smouldering logs.

In a reflex action, he'd used his arm to lever himself out of harm's way. But he hadn't been quick enough. In seconds, the tight sleeve of his track top had become as lethal as one of the burning logs.

'Oh, my lord!' Joanna's stomach lurched sickeningly.

In one fluid movement, Matt was on his feet, tipping her almost bodily off the rug. 'Get my bag!' He thrust his keys at her. 'Grab everything you think we'll need, Joanna. Hurry!'

Amongst the cries of disbelief, Matt's voice rose authoritatively. 'Get him on the ground and roll him!' In a second Scott was lying on the grass and Matt had thrown the blanket over him to stop the insidious creep of the flame. 'Deb...' He swung his gaze up, his gut tightening. His sister's face was rucked with fear. 'Grab the garden hose,' he said urgently. 'We need water on Scott's burns.'

Debra made a little moan in her throat and ran.

Bent on her own mission, Joanna moved like lightning, running to where Matt had parked his car. He'd said he was well equipped for emergencies. She only hoped he was.

She yanked open the boot of his Mercedes, her gaze flying over the contents. From the little she'd seen, they had a real emergency on their hands. They didn't have a second to spare. She took a steadying breath, reaching into the boot to snatch up Matt's medical case, a space blanket and what was obviously a standby trauma kit.

Please, God, she implored silently, let us not be looking at a tragedy...

Matt had called for calm and the guests had drawn into a hushed little group. He looked up and acknowledged Joanna briefly as she dropped down beside him.

'How bad is it?' Joanna felt her mouth dry.

'Pretty bad.' Matt was grim. 'Let's get him on oxygen. He's going into shock fast.'

Joanna delved into the trauma kit for what they'd need. A powerful torch came out first, and she swung the light across so Matt could see what he was doing. One glance told them the synthetic material from Scott's top had melted like butter on his flesh all the way to his shoulder.

'Oh, my God!' Deb burst out, her voice reedy with apprehension. 'He said he had a headache earlier. He couldn't have looked where he was treading—'

'Take it easy, Deb.' Matt was gentle. 'We'll do everything we can.'

'But he must be in such pain.'

'I'm about to give him something now.' Joanna moved swiftly to cannulate Scott, realising they'd need to run fluids through the line as well as the drugs. 'Is Scott allergic to anything?'

Deb shook her head. 'No—not that we know of. Oh, God, Matt…' Her hand went to her throat, the gravity of her husband's situation taking hold. 'He's—not going to die, is he?'

'No, he's not!' Matt responded clearly, and hoped he wasn't lying through his teeth. 'Deb, I know it's hard, just watching, but if you want to be helpful, could you get us some wet towels? We'll need to keep Scott's skin hydrated on the way to the hospital.'

'I'll help.' Elle, who had unobtrusively joined the group, took Debra's arm and turned her quickly in the direction of the house.

'IV's in and holding.' Joanna's tone was crisp. 'I've put up five hundred mils of fluids. And I'd like to go with morphine five milligrams and Maxolon ten. Sound about right?'

Matt nodded. 'Thanks, Joanna.' His expression tightened. Where he'd been able to, he'd cut away the burned remnants of Scott's top. He shook his head.

There were still minute particles adhering to the skin and it was going to take a surgeon, using special solvents and fine scalpels, to remove them. Scott was in for a long haul.

Following his gaze, Joanna made a little sound of distress. 'Burns are such cruel injuries.'

'I wouldn't wish them on my worst enemy.' Swiftly, he made a check of Scott's blood pressure. 'Hell's bells.' He frowned at the reading. 'He's going into rapid shock! Put up more fluids, please, Joanna. We have to hold him somehow. And hit him with another two milligrams of morph!'

The ambulance arrived and things began moving quickly. 'Sorry about this, folks,' Matt addressed the guests grimly. 'Would you mind seeing yourselves off?'

'No worries, Doc.' One of the men had begun dousing the fire.

'Will Scott be all right?' Several of the women drew closer.

The lines of strain etched deeper around Matt's mouth. 'Let's hope so.'

Joanna touched his arm. 'Will you go with Scott in the ambulance?'

He nodded. 'By the look of things, I'll have to intubate him on the way.'

'Tricky.' Joanna drew in a shaken breath. 'Want me to come with you?'

'Thanks, but no.' Matt rubbed a finger across his forehead. 'But I'd be grateful if you'd look after Deb. She'll want to be at the hospital. Take my car.'

'What about the boys?'

Matt looked torn. 'They went to bed ages ago...'

'I'll stay,' Elle offered. 'Please, heaven, things will be looking much better by the morning.'

'I'm sorry your evening's been ruined, Joanna,' Deb said for the umpteenth time, as they sat in the hospital waiting room. 'And Matt's, too.'

'Deb, please.' Joanna gave the other woman's hand a comforting squeeze. 'Just be thankful we were there for Scott and we could act promptly.' Joanna stole a glance at her watch, wondering just how much longer Matt was going to be. He'd insisted on speaking to the surgeon, telling Deb he'd be back when he had something concrete to tell her.

She could only hope and pray the outcome for Scott would be positive.

'Scott's going to be terribly scarred, isn't he?' Deb said with a little catch in her voice. 'Tell me truthfully, Joanna, is there a chance he could lose his arm?'

Joanna hid her unease. The truth was, she had no way of knowing the full extent of Scott's injuries. She only knew the burns had gone very deep, but whether they had destroyed vital muscles and tissue... 'Deb, I know it's awful just waiting, but the management of burn injuries has come on in leaps and bounds.'

'I suppose so.' Deb's face worked for a minute.

Joanna sought to be positive. 'Immediately Scott was brought in, he'd have been monitored for the slightest problem. And specialised burn dressings would have been applied to give his damaged skin every chance of survival.' Joanna firmed her grip on the other's hand. 'Please, don't dwell on the worst-case scenario. Look, why don't I get us a cup of coffee?'

Deb nodded. 'OK...thanks, Joanna.'

'I'll take an extra minute to ring my son.' Joanna got to her feet. 'Just to let him know where I am.'

Knowing the use of mobile phones within the hospital precincts was banned, Joanna slid her money into the payphone and dialled her home number. Jason answered promptly, and she explained what had happened.

'Will...Mr Carlisle be OK?'

Joanna heard the youthful uncertainty. 'We're hoping so. Matt should be back any minute from speaking with the surgeon. I'll be home as soon as I can, Jase.'

'Yeah, no worries, Mum. I'll watch telly for a while.'

'Don't stay up too late,' Joanna cautioned, and then wished she hadn't. Just lately she'd begun to realise her son wasn't a child any more. And if anything were to come of her relationship with Matt McKellar, that was something else she'd have to be very aware of.

Seeing Debra so strung out and pinched-looking when she returned with the coffee, it made Joanna feel suddenly guilty for having allowed her own selfish needs to take over, even for a minute.

As they sipped their coffee, both women were silent, each occupied with their own thoughts. Finally Deb stirred. 'Will Matt know where to find us? Sorry.' She made a small face. 'It's just that the waiting seems endless.'

'Deb, I know,' Joanna commiserated softly. 'But I'm sure Matt will get here just as soon as he has something to tell us.' She lifted her head and stiffened slightly, Matt McKellar's approach making something odd happen inside her chest. 'Look.' She touched Deb's shoulder. 'Here he is now.'

'Oh, thank heaven!' In a second, Debra had dumped her coffee, moving awkwardly between the chairs towards Matt's tall figure.

Watching brother and sister, their dark heads close together, Joanna felt suddenly in the way. But she couldn't leave until she at least had some knowledge of Scott's condition...

She'd waited. Matt couldn't believe the joy he felt just seeing her there. And with quiet honesty, he faced the fact that Joanna Winters had already crept right under his skin. And what a hell of a time to be having these kinds of crazy thoughts, he derided himself, guiding Debra across to where Joanna waited.

Joanna managed a half-smile, her heart leaping anew at the sight of him, watching as he pulled out a chair so that they sat in a semi-circle.

'So, how is Scott and what's the prognosis?' Joanna asked quietly, itching to reach out and touch his hand where it lay across his thigh.

'Scott's in Theatre now,' Matt began carefully, and looked at his sister. 'He's in for a long old op, Deb. But Jon Barkley, the surgeon, is hopeful of a good outcome.'

'Oh...' Deb sagged against him. 'Thank heavens. I'd begun thinking all kinds of crazy things.'

'Come on, Deb,' her brother cajoled bracingly, 'you won't lose Scott. But he's in for a bumpy ride over the next few months.'

'They'll do skin grafts?' Joanna's dark brows lifted in question.

Matt nodded. 'From the thigh initially. But it's quite probable they'll need to send Scott on to the burns unit at the Royal in Brisbane for future management.'

'That all sounds very positive.' Suddenly, Joanna was on her feet, deciding she didn't want to intrude any further in what was clearly now a time for family. The repercussions from Scott's accident would be many and there were domestic decisions and arrangements that would have to be made. 'If there's nothing else I can do, I'll find a cab, I think, and get off home.'

'I'll walk out with you.' There was a taut edge to Matt's voice and his gaze skimmed over her discerningly. He frowned a bit. She must be out on her feet.

'Joanna…' Deb brought her head up. 'Thanks for, well, everything. I'm so grateful…'

Joanna swallowed hard on the tightness in her throat. 'No thanks needed, Deb.' She bent and squeezed the other's shoulder, then turned and began walking quickly towards the exit.

Matt was right beside her.

'Will you be all right?' He pushed through the entrance doors and drew her to a halt in the shadowy light outside.

'I'll be fine.' Joanna brushed a strand of hair back from her temple. 'I left your car in the doctors' car park and Deb has the keys.'

'Thanks.' A muscle flickered in his jaw as he raised his hands to curve them around her shoulders, leaving her no option but to look at him. 'I feel as though I've short-changed you this evening, Joanna. I should've been taking you home. Instead…'

'I know…' She drew a shaky breath. 'But you have to stay with your sister, Matt. Just let's pray Scott recovers quickly.'

'Yes. I was damned glad to have your help this evening.' His hand shifted to brush across her cheek. 'But you're right,' he added ruefully. 'I'll have to stay with Deb. There's no way she'll go home until she's checked on Scott.'

'No.' Joanna's response was automatic. Her mind flew ahead and she wondered when she'd see Matt again. Would it be soon or would he be all tied up, helping Debra sort out her immediate problem? But somehow she knew she would see him. 'Matt...' Suddenly, she could almost feel the tension vibrating between them, shakenly recognising her own riot of emotions. 'I should go.'

'I know you should...but I don't want you to...'

His husky tones lapped at the edge of her resistance and she felt him draw her closer. Confusion and want shimmered across her eyes at the realisation he was going to kiss her—and she gave in to the desire that she wanted him to. Needed him to. She breathed in, the musky scent of his cologne stirring her senses, sending shivers all along her spine.

Her eyelids fluttered down and she felt the touch of his lips on hers, tasting her, until she opened her mouth to his. He made a sound in his throat, accepting her invitation to deepen the kiss, exploring the softness of her lips with a tenderness that was utterly sweet.

After the longest time, his mouth left hers and he stroked her hair. 'Come.' His chest lifted in a long sigh. 'I'll see you safely into a cab.'

It was the following Saturday before she saw him again.

That morning, after Jason had left for work, Joanna

had thrown her energies into the housework and had just finished cleaning the oven—a job she'd decided she'd put off for too long—when the doorbell rang. And rang again.

'All right, all right,' she muttered, tugging off her rubber gloves and tossing them into the sink. 'Coming,' she called, puffing a wayward strand of hair from her forehead as she made her way along the hallway to the front door.

'Yes, what is it?' She flung open the door, expecting to see a local child brandishing some school raffle tickets or whatever. 'Matt...' she said softly, flustered.

'Bad timing?' He gave a mocking lift to his eyebrows, his gaze homing in on her hand clutching the neckline of her faded T-shirt.

'Well, you've just missed the oven-cleaning.' She gave a stilted laugh to cover her embarrassment. 'So, from your point of view, it's probably good timing.' She stood back to let him in.

'I should've rung, perhaps?'

'No—it's fine. Honestly.' Joanna had seen his look of uncertainty and hastened to put him at ease. 'Come through.' She led the way to the kitchen. 'I've a couple of chores to tidy away. Coffee?'

'Ah.' Matt gave a crooked smile and followed her. 'I wondered if you'd like to have lunch actually.'

'Lunch.' Joanna stared at him, bemused.

'Yes—you know, as in go to the pub and order a glass of wine and some food and so on.'

'Um...yes...OK, then.'

Noticing her slight hesitation, he frowned. 'Am I treading on anyone's toes here, Joanna?'

'Toes?'

His hand reached out briefly to snag her wrist. 'I've been assuming you're not committed.' His gaze slanted over her, a question in his eyes, and a brief smile touched his mouth. 'I think that's the politically correct term they use now, isn't it?'

'I'm not.' She shook her head, looking down to where his hand curved over her wrist. His touch had had a strange effect on her, a sensation of instant fire that raced through her bloodstream. 'Only to my son, of course,' she added softly.

'I understand. So, then, Dr Winters…' Matt drew her hand up and playfully rubbed her knuckles across his chin. 'We can do lunch?'

'We can.' She shook her hair back and laughed shakily. 'I just need a few minutes to shower and change.'

'You've got it.' Matt crinkled a smile and let her hand go.

'The weekend papers are in the lounge.' Joanna turned away, hastily aiming some bits and pieces at the bin and then straightened towards him. 'Make yourself comfortable. I won't be long.'

She threw herself under the shower, aware her heart was revving. And when she was dressed, she felt like a girl again in her snug-fitting jeans and sleek little ribbed jumper. She bit back a startled laugh. She looked good. And she had a lunch date with a very handsome man.

With an impatient flick of his wrist, Matt dropped the copy of the *Weekend Australian* back on to the coffee table. He may as well have been reading it upside down for all he'd taken in.

He blew out a long breath, standing abruptly and

pacing across to the window. His hands in the pockets of his jungle-green chinos, he peered out at the garden bed of mauve and white flowers that ran along the inside of the brick fence. He didn't know what they were called but their perfume as he'd come through the gate had been heady with a distinctive spicy smell.

And why on earth was he wittering on, albeit silently about flowers, when in reality his mind couldn't get past Joanna Winters and the powerful effect she was having on his equilibrium?

His expression became shuttered, blade-sharp desire hitting him out of nowhere. Hell! He clenched his hands in his pockets. His stomach felt tied in knots, as though a very bad surgeon had been let loose on his guts...

Where do you think you're going with this? Joanna stared into her dressing-table mirror, as if demanding an answer from her wide-eyed reflection. Suddenly, reality in the form of a prowling Matt McKellar just inches away beyond the dividing wall had set up a hard knot of uncertainty in her stomach. She drew in a quivery breath, automatically settling a lock of hair behind her ear. She'd allowed herself to open up to Matt because it had felt so natural, so right. But in doing so, had she left herself even more vulnerable?

For a long time now, she'd been content to let her life jog along with Jason at its centre. But now her life was changing even as she stood here. Because now a new player had entered the stage. Now, there was Matt McKellar...

CHAPTER FOUR

'ANYWHERE in particular you'd like to eat?' Matt slid the car smoothly away from the kerb.

'I'm easy.' Joanna cringed inwardly. What a pathetic way to have expressed herself.

'The Federal serves a reasonable counter lunch.' Matt sent her a fleeting look. 'Shall we try there?'

'Fine with me.' Joanna's teeth caught her bottom lip. Suddenly, she felt unaccountably nervous, out of kilter. 'How is Scott doing?' she asked into the growing silence between them.

'Well, it's only been a week.' Matt gave a twitch of his shoulder. 'Progress is understandably slow but the consultant is sure they'll save the arm.'

'How is Deb managing?'

He frowned. 'She's determined to keep their programmes going at Featherdale. At the moment she's being assisted by a couple of students from the agricultural college. They're classing it as work experience. And I'll keep an eye on things where I can.'

Joanna knotted her fingers together in her lap. 'I did phone the hospital to enquire about Scott but got only the standard reply. And I didn't want to intrude on Deb—'

'You could have called me.'

She felt a little rush of colour flood her cheeks, mentally fending off the mild rebuke. It wasn't justified anyway. She *had* thought about ringing Matt.

Endlessly. She'd even lifted the receiver once, only to slam it down, recoiling as the nerves in her stomach had gathered and clenched as though they'd been attached to a thousand fine wires.

Her head went back on the soft leather. 'I meant to. I wanted to, but...'

'You sat looking at the phone instead.'

'Snap.'

His mouth kicked up in a wry smile. 'For intelligent people, we let the craziest things faze us, don't we?'

Joanna smothered a smile. 'You, too?'

'You bet. All the time. Should I? Shouldn't I?'

'I expect we're afraid of making fools of ourselves. Or perhaps we're just afraid...'

Matt grinned. 'I'd settle for plain wimping out.'

'Well, I'm glad you didn't wimp out today,' she said softly, turning to meet his gaze, as they halted for a set of traffic lights.

'Me, too,' Matt replied, his tone gruff.

Joanna took a shaken breath. In the few seconds while they waited for the signal to turn green, he reached across and took her wrist, his thumb massaging her pulse point almost absently. Within the space of a heartbeat the whole of her arm was tingling, the dizzying feeling winging all the way to her backbone and beyond.

'I haven't been here before.' Joanna cast her gaze around the pleasant surrounds of the hotel, taking in the soft colours of the décor, the patina of old timber furniture, the glow from the copper pans used as decorative features behind the bar.

'There's a blackboard menu.' Matt placed a guiding hand at her waist. 'I gather you're hungry?' He sent her a fleeting grin.

'A bit,' she understated. 'Housework seems to do that to me.' But even as she made the light-hearted remark, Joanna's throat was tightening and she doubted whether she'd be able to swallow anything.

'The fish is usually good.' Thoughtfully, Matt stroked a finger across his chin. 'Whiting skewers with ginger and soy. Sound OK?'

'Lovely.' She gave him a shaky smile.

Their fish came with an Asian salad, and with the warming effect of a rather dry white wine, Joanna began to relax and enjoy her meal. 'I wish I were a more adventurous cook,' she lamented, tasting the fresh tang of lime juice in the salad dressing.

'It takes time and practice,' Matt responded evenly. 'And I don't imagine you've much of the former.'

'Possibly not.' Joanna paused, picking up her wineglass and looking at him. 'What about you, Matt? Do you like to cook?'

He smiled, a mere sensual curving of his lips. 'Will you dump me if I say no?'

'It's a possibility.' His low, suggestively teasing comment had her thoughts whirling giddily, and for a moment it seemed as if life had snatched her up and begun propelling her too fast into a wide uncertain future.

'I can do a simple meal.' His tone was softly wry. 'And I always keep a large packet of cornflakes in the pantry for when I'm not more inspired.'

'Back-up,' she murmured through a throaty laugh. 'Very wise. You make good coffee anyway.'

'Ah…' He made a face. 'Gracie Storer, our cleaner at the club, usually does all that before she leaves for the day.'

Joanna clicked her tongue and laughed again. 'You don't have much going for you at all, then, Dr McKellar.'

'Then let's thank heaven, you do, Dr Winters.' Matt spoke softly, leaning across to trap her hand between his palm and the soft fabric of the tablecloth. 'So, what are we going to do about it?'

She swallowed unevenly, her suddenly downcast lashes fanning darkly across her cheekbones. 'I…don't understand what you're asking…'

'Come and work with me.' He released her hand and sat back in his chair, regarding her through narrowed eyes.

Her lashes flew up. 'But I know nothing about delivering sports medicine,' she forced out jerkily.

'I'd be your mentor,' he said, his blue eyes fixed on her. 'With some intensive training, we could cover everything you'd need to know within a reasonable time span. You have much of the background anyway.' He lifted a shoulder dismissively. 'It's just a matter of reactivating everything you were taught about physiology in med school and combining it with some specialised know-how. And I'd always be around for back-up.'

Joanna blinked. His proposition had come out of nowhere, leaving her confused, startled. 'Why me?'

'Why not you?' Matt had quietly resumed his meal. 'The centre urgently needs another doctor, more particularly a female doctor. And from what I've seen so far, you have the qualities we need. You were quick and intuitive at Scott's accident. You didn't dither. You went in boots and all. And you have a natural empathy with people.'

Well, it was all very flattering. Joanna moistened her lips. 'What if I said I was interested?'

'I go with a recommendation to the board and that's it. You're in.' He named a salary that left her head spinning.

'Heavens!' Her hands shook slightly as she locked them around the stem of her glass and gazed across at his bent dark head. 'That seems unusually generous.'

'It's the going rate.'

'What if I made a mess of it?'

'You wouldn't, Joanna. I'd see to that.'

Joanna blinked through a long pause. 'What kind of hours would I be required to work?'

'Different, I'd guess, from what you presently work as a GP.' Matt placed his knife and fork neatly together on his plate. 'But more flexible.'

And that meant she'd possibly see more of her son. Joanna ran a finger around the base of her glass, admitting that even though at the back of her mind she'd been toying with the idea of moving on from general practice, this proposition from Matt had placed an urgency on her decision.

'How long do I have to think about it?' she asked.

'Not long.' His look sharpened and then he grinned. 'What about a coffee in the meantime?'

Surely he was joking? He couldn't expect her to give him an answer in five minutes—even in five days! She'd need to give the idea much more thought. Yet, rationally, what was there to think about? her inner voice urged. Either you want a career change or you don't. But I might hate working with him, she reasoned.

Well, isn't it better to find out now than—?

'Coffee for two.' Matt placed the cups on the table.

'Hi, Mum.'

Joanna jumped guiltily, her fingers tightening involuntarily on the pile of laundry she'd been sorting. 'Jason...' she smiled a bit awkwardly. 'I was miles away. How was work?'

'OK.' The youth slammed his push-bike against the wall of the laundry. 'Where were you at lunchtime?'

'Lunchtime?' Joanna felt a dull flush crawl up her throat and over her cheekbones.

Jason tugged off his stack-hat and tossed it onto the bench. 'I tried to call you in my break. Daniel asked if I'd like to go to Speedway at Calverston tonight. His dad got some tickets through his work. I called you to check it was OK.'

Joanna knew it was time to be honest with her son about her growing involvement with Matt, but she stalled for time. 'Wasn't the answering machine on?'

Jason shook his head.

'I must have forgotten. Actually, Matt called by and asked me to lunch.' Hastily, she resumed folding the freshly laundered towels.

The boy set his head at an enquiring angle. 'Why'd he do that?'

Joanna's mind emptied. 'Um...we enjoy each other's company, I suppose, and it seemed a nice thing to do.' Her resolve firmed. 'I'm sorry I wasn't

here to get your call, Jase, but you know it's usually
OK for you to go with Daniel and his dad to things…'

'Yeah…well…' Jason set his mouth in a mutinous
line. 'You always say I should ask.'

Sighing inwardly, Joanna picked up the basket of
towels for despatch to the linen cupboard. Obviously
they needed to clear the air. Just lately too much had
been left simmering. And she certainly didn't want
things to develop into a confrontation with her son.
She sent him a quick smile. 'Let's go inside, love. I
want to talk to you.'

In the quiet cosiness of the kitchen, they sat over
mugs of steaming chocolate. Joanna took a deep
breath, moistening her lips before addressing her son.
'Matt's asked me to join the staff at the sports clinic.'

Jason's eyes flicked up and locked with his
mother's, so like her own in every way. 'Why would
you want to do that? You like working at the
Strachan, don't you?'

Joanna bristled at his assumption that her work situation was everything she wished for and at having
to explain herself to her child. 'As a matter of fact,
I've been thinking of making a change. I didn't know
to quite what but then Matt made his offer. And it's
genuine,' she reinforced, as Jason gave her an old-
fashioned look from suddenly widened eyes.

Joanna sighed abruptly. 'I thought you'd be
pleased. The hours would be much more flexible and
I wouldn't have to leave you on your own so much.'

Jason made an irritated hissing sound between his
lips. 'Mum, I'm sixteen, not six!'

'All the more reason for you to understand that I
might just possibly want a change in my work envi-

ronment,' she snapped, and then relented. 'You like Matt, don't you?'

'So what?' Jason lifted a shoulder. 'Doesn't mean I want you working for him.'

'I wouldn't be working *for* him,' she explained patiently. 'I'd be part of the medical team. And I have to tell you, Jase, at this moment I find the idea challenging and exciting.'

'So, go work for him, then!' The boy shot up off the chair and glowered down at his mother. 'Do what you want. You don't need *my* permission,' he added sarcastically, and slammed out of the room, banging the door shut so hard the frame all but shook.

Joanna swung round, tempted to call him back but resisting the impulse. Instead, she sat chewing her lip, her face stiff with hurt and puzzlement. What had so upset her son for him to have acted so drastically out of character? After a long moment the penny dropped and she sat in frozen unbelief.

He was jealous.

Jealous because their cosy twosome was suddenly under threat. And the fact that the catalyst was Matt McKellar had somehow seemed to inflame the situation.

Well, at least it had sorted things out in her mind. The realisation came like an arrow winging to its target. Joanna rose decisively to her feet. She'd call Matt tomorrow and tell him she'd take the job and on Monday she'd give in her notice at the Strachan clinic.

And last, but not least, Jason would have to learn to accept that things in the Winters household were about to change.

But even with her decision made, Joanna couldn't relax that evening.

Earlier, Jason had mumbled an apology which she'd accepted and he'd gone out to Speedway with Daniel. But the atmosphere between them was far from clear.

When Jason had left, she ran a bath, intending to have a long, lazy soak, but that didn't work out. A strange restlessness came over her so that in the end she cut her bath short and went to bed with a book, leaving the lounge light on for Jason.

Sunday came and went and, despite her resolution to phone Matt, Joanna couldn't bring herself to make the call. To make matters worse, she'd begun to experience a lingering sense of unreality about his job offer. Was she really ready for the changes its acceptance would make in her life?

And it was pointless trying to discuss things with Jason. He'd more or less shut down, being unusually subdued and attending to his homework without being chivvied along. Joanna frowned. That fact alone was only adding to her uncertainty.

She was still no nearer a plan of action when she parked her car outside the Strachan clinic on Monday morning. She stifled a sigh, swinging out of the car and locking it. Lifting her head, she gave a cursory look around. Her shoulders rose in a little shrug. Everything looked the same despite the fact her own world was in turmoil.

Well, this isn't getting the working day started, she berated herself. Determinedly marching around to the boot of her car, she opened it and hauled out her medical case, which seemed to be getting heavier every week, she thought wryly. These days, there appeared to be a newer or faster-acting drug sample to be tucked into any spare corner.

Pasting on a smile, she pushed her way in through Reception. 'Morning, Steffi. Nice weekend?' she enquired of the receptionist, and then wished immediately she hadn't been so quick off the mark with the glib Monday morning question. Steffi was the sole carer for her mother whose diabetes was progressively worsening. Joanna suspected the young woman's weekend had been anything but nice.

'Thanks,' she murmured, taking the pile of patient cards Steffi held out to her and noticing the sad little droop to the young woman's mouth and the dark smudges under her eyes. 'Want to talk, Stef?' Homing in on the other's demeanour, Joanna's invitation was spontaneous.

Steffi gave a cracked laugh. 'I knew I should've slapped on more make-up.'

'Come through where we'll be private.' Joanna's touch on the younger woman's arm was firm.

Steffi swallowed. 'Do you have time?' She hastily dipped her head to try to hide the bright glimmer of tears.

But Joanna had seen anyway. 'I'm disgustingly early,' she said lightly. 'Coffee made?'

Steffi gave a wobbly smile and nodded.

'Then let's play hookey.' Joanna gave a conspiratorial smile. 'Switch the phones over to the answering machine and we'll have a natter over coffee, shall we? I know I could do with a sympathetic ear,' she added ruefully. 'My son's hardly speaking to me.'

*   *   *

'Oh, that's good.' Joanna had taken several long mouthfuls of her coffee and now leaned back in her chair. She and Steffi had made themselves comfortable at the small cane setting near the window. She stifled a giggle and looked around her. 'You know, I've never worked in such a large consulting room before now.'

'Well, they can afford it.' The receptionist lifted a shoulder dismissively. 'They're not exactly free with the salary rises.'

'You've had a rotten weekend, haven't you?' Joanna asked quietly. 'How's your mum doing?'

Steffi bit her lip. 'The glaucoma is getting worse. She can't see properly to draw up her insulin any more. I have to make sure I'm there to administer it. But at least her leg ulcer has improved. Di Anderson, the community nurse, has been wonderful. Mum really looks forward to her visits.'

'Well, that's good.' Looking across at Steffi, Joanna's gaze sharpened professionally. Worry and strain were ingrained on the young woman's face. 'But what about you, Stef?' she asked. 'How are you coping?'

'Oh, you know…' Steffi's mouth trembled slightly, before she raised her mug and gulped at her coffee. 'I'll be twenty-five soon,' she bit out. 'And what have I got to look forward to? A night in with my mum! Another year of not having an hour to call my own.' She stopped, hastily scrabbling for a tissue in her pocket and dabbing at her eyes. 'Sorry.' She hiccuped a laugh. 'I'm being pathetic…'

'No, you're not!' Joanna felt her own problems

pale into insignificance. Steffi looked at the end of her rope. Joanna delved into her mind for possible solutions. 'What about some respite care for your mum?'

Steffi shook her head. 'That's just pie in the sky, Joanna. You know that.'

Joanna did. As in most of the ancillary areas of medicine, there were never enough volunteers to meet the requirements of the community. And funding was stretched to the limits. 'You have a sister, don't you?'

'Alex.' Steffi nodded. 'She tries to help but she lives out of town and she has a young family.'

'No chance your mum could go to her and give you a break?'

Steffi shrugged. 'Mum likes her own space.'

Well, that seemed to be that. Joanna felt hamstrung. Abruptly, she swung off her chair and moved to the window, staring out. Her index finger tapped against her chin as she set her mind to work, seeking a solution for Steffi.

'Actually, Joanna, I, uh, could do with a bit of professional advice, if you have the time.'

Joanna turned and blinked. Steffi had her auburn head bent, her hands clasped tightly in front of her.

'Sure.' Joanna made her tone casual. 'Fire away.'

Steffi's shoulders rose in a controlling breath. 'Sometimes...I wonder just how I'm going to keep on going...'

'How long have you been feeling like this?' Joanna's head came up in query.

'A while now. I, um, try to just get on with it when I'm here at work, but then I go home and everything crowds in and I'm snappy with Mum. It's like a vicious circle.'

'Do you have tightness in your chest?'

Steffi took a shuddering breath. 'A bit—sometimes.'

'Periods OK?' Joanna asked. 'Not unduly heavy or anything?'

'Cramps now and again. But I'm regular with my pap smears.'

'Hop up on the couch for me. I'll feel your tummy and then I'll take your BP. We may as well run a blood test while we're at it.'

Joanna's examination was thorough.

'So, how am I?' Steffi asked.

'Everything seems normal.' Joanna released the blood-pressure cuff. 'But you're very tense.' She looked thoughtful for a moment. 'How would you feel about taking a mild antidepressant?'

'I suppose…' Steffi looked hesitant. Pulling herself upright, she dangled her legs over the edge of the couch. 'Would they become addictive?'

'Not if we keep an eye on you.' Joanna went back to her desk and took her prescription pad from its drawer. 'And possibly you need only take them to ease you over this rough patch.'

'Would there be any side effects?' Steffi slipped her shoes back on and sat opposite Joanna.

'Not with this particular one.' Joanna smiled and handed the script to the younger woman. 'And come and talk to me, Steffi,' she emphasised. 'Sometimes just talking things through helps enormously.'

Steffi nodded and bit her lip. 'Thanks, Joanna—for listening and everything.'

'No thanks necessary.' Joanna flapped a hand dismissively. 'Check in with me if you've any concerns at all. If not, we'll chat again in a couple of weeks and see how you're going. And about your period cramps, you might like to try hot and cold herbal baths to improve your circulation. It's a bit old-fashioned but often effective.'

With another murmured word of thanks, Steffi got to her feet. 'Oh.' she turned at the door, clutching the script to her chest, a pained look on her face. 'You mentioned Jason earlier. I was so caught up with myself, I forgot to ask. Is there a problem?'

Joanna sent her a crooked smile. 'Just a bit of teenage angst,' she understated. 'I'm sure it'll pass.'

And why don't I believe that for a second? she asked herself silently. Sighing a little, she gathered up their used coffee-mugs and made her way to the kitchen. And then her patients began to arrive in a steady trickle and she had no more time to indulge in semantics concerning her son's present attitude.

By four o'clock, Joanna realised that for the whole day she hadn't had a chance to think about Matt or his job offer. But perhaps she should call him now, she thought, and with the possibility of hearing his voice every nerve in her body tightened. Oh, lord, what should she do? Make a decision, that's what, she thought dismally, propping her head in her hands to massage a dull ache across her temple.

A rap sounded on her door.

'Yes, come in.' Joanna hastily schooled her expression.

'Got a minute to see me?' Kim Newlands, a rep

for one of the drug companies, shoved his fair crew-cut around the door.

Joanna stifled a groan. 'If you're here to try to flog me anything, you're dead,' she warned him.

'Ouch!' He stepped back, his hand on his heart, and then grinned disarmingly. 'Save your fire, Doc. I'm here as a patient. I leant on Steffi.'

'Used your charm on her more likely,' Joanna responded dryly, waving him to a chair.

'Steffi said your last appointment cancelled,' he said cheerfully. 'You should be glad I'm here to make up your quota.'

Joanna all but rolled her eyes. 'What can I do for you, Kim?'

'I'm feeling knackered all the time,' he said bluntly. 'I've recently had to make two international trips. They were hellishly long flights and now I find my sleep pattern's all over the place. That's when I *can* sleep. I wondered if you could give me something to knock me out.'

Joanna clicked her tongue. 'That's not a long-term solution, Kim. Your circadian rhythm is probably still out of sync.'

'Tell me about it.' He rammed a hand through the low bristles of his hairstyle. 'What should I do, then, Joanna? I'm useless. Haven't been on a date for weeks,' he lamented with a crooked grin.

'Poor you.' Joanna found herself grinning back at him as she leaned across to take his blood pressure. She'd known Kim since she'd come to the Strachan. He'd even asked her out once but she hadn't gone, deeming him too young for her. 'That seems fine.' She released the blood-pressure cuff and placed it to one side. 'Ideally, you should try to go to bed at the same time each night,' she told him.

His smile was rueful. 'Well, I suppose I can do that.'

'And have a hot drink,' Joanna continued. 'Try one of the herbal teas.'

Kim made a face. 'What about a slug of Scotch?'

Joanna ignored the suggestion. 'Try all the usual things as well, like having only a light meal in the evening, a warm bath, relaxing music—'

'And sip my tea,' he slipped in cheekily.

'Or warm milk.'

'With a dash of brandy?'

'Oh, for heaven's sake!' Joanna tsked. 'Stop fooling around, Kim. Do you want my professional advice or not?'

He looked suitably chastened. 'I'll do what you've suggested, Doc. But what if it doesn't work? I'll go nuts.'

'You can't rush it,' she warned. 'Take it slowly and eventually your normal sleep pattern will re-establish itself with local time. But realise the more it has been disrupted, the longer it may take.'

'OK. I'll give it a go.' Languidly, he raised his arms and stretched. 'So—how're things with you, Joey? Not married again yet?'

'They're fine and, no, I'm not.' Joanna began to tidy things on her desk. 'What about you?'

He shrugged. 'No luck yet meeting the right woman. I'll be thirty this year.'

'That's terribly ancient.' The smile was hard to suppress. 'But no doubt your soul mate is out there somewhere.'

'Yours, too?' he asked softly.

She felt the blush creep up her cheeks. 'Who knows?' she said primly, but he just chuckled. And he seemed in no hurry to leave either! She looked pointedly at her watch.

'Steffi's a honey, isn't she?' Kim pushed his chair back, crossing one leg so that his ankle rested on his opposite knee.

Thrown by his sudden change of topic, Joanna gave a guarded smile. 'She is. And very good at her job. I don't know what we'd do without her.'

Kim arched a dark-fair brow. 'Does she have a boyfriend?'

'Not that I know of.' Joanna was startled into a reply. 'Why?'

Kim lifted a shoulder. 'I've asked her out a few times. She's always backed off. I just wondered...'

'Steffi has an invalid mother.' Joanna felt sure she wasn't betraying a confidence. The whole of the staff knew of Steffi's domestic situation.

'She could get someone to sit with her, though, couldn't she?'

'Perhaps.' A wild idea was beginning to form in Joanna's mind. She'd done nothing but dither about her own love life, it couldn't hurt to give Steffi's a shove in the right direction. And for all his nonsense, Kim was a nice man. And fun. And right now Steffi needed a dose of light-hearted male company almost as much as her own breathing.

'I was beginning to think I had a personal hygiene problem,' Kim said cheerfully. 'But if it's only a case of—'

'Ask her out again,' Joanna broke in urgently. 'But

not today. I may know of someone to sit with her mum…'

'And that would ease the way for Steffi to say yes,' Kim finished with a wide grin. 'When should I ask her, then? Give me a time span.'

Joanna thought quickly. 'Give it a while yet. I happen to know Steffi has a birthday coming up as well. Maybe if her mum's taken care of, that could be the impetus for Stef to go out with you.' She grinned across at him. 'What do you think?'

'I think you're brilliant, Dr Winters. Amazingly, bloody well brilliant.' Kim was all smiles as he left.

For the first time in her life Joanna was almost reluctant to go home. And with the realisation came a sudden pang of guilt.

But the fact was, she'd have to face Jason again and heaven knew what kind of mood he'd be in. Kids, she thought. Why was it such an uphill battle?

Putting off the inevitable, she did some grocery shopping at her local supermarket and then drove slowly home along the tree-lined street.

Pulling into the driveway, she cut the engine and swung out of the car. 'Jason!' She almost collided with her son as he jumped down from the rockery and stood awkwardly beside her on the concrete driveway.

'Want a hand with anything?'

'Please, love.' Joanna's smile spelt relief. 'Groceries in the boot. If you'd take them inside, I'll put the car away.'

'No worries.' Jason picked up the plastic bags as

though they were filled with feathers and loped through the carport towards the back door.

Thoughtfully, Joanna nosed the car under cover. Jason appeared to be in high spirits. Perhaps she'd been right after all and his mood over the weekend *had* been merely a fit of teenage angst. But whatever had wrought the change back to his normal easygoing self, she welcomed it with open arms.

'I got some of that Turkish bread you like,' she told him, and together they began to unpack the contents of the grocery bags.

'Cool.' His grin was infectious. 'Can we do some steak sandwiches for dinner?'

'Sure, why not? As long we make a salad to go with them,' Joanna stipulated. 'You seem in a good mood,' she added lightly.

'I'm in the firsts for the athletic team for the all-schools comp.'

Joanna paused with the bottle of wine she'd slid from its wrapping. 'Hey, that's brilliant!'

'I reckon.' Jason was grinning broadly. 'Dad was good at athletics, wasn't he?'

Joanna sobered for a second. 'Your dad was a natural at all sports, Jase. You're very like him.'

Jason crossed his trainer-clad feet and leant back against the bench top. 'I thought we could dig out his old school photos tonight. Especially the ones where he was captain of the rugger team.'

Joanna lifted a shoulder. 'If you'd like to.' She turned her head as the doorbell sounded. 'Get that, please, Jase? I'll make a start on dinner.'

Going to the fridge, Joanna took a cos lettuce from the crisper and began to separate the leaves into a metal basket ready for washing. Intent on her task, she didn't hear the front door close. But suddenly the echo of firm footsteps in the hallway had her tilting her head towards the sound. Oh, lord, she sighed inwardly, she just wasn't in the mood for visitors.

Grabbing a strip of paper towel, she dried her hands, looking up just as a male figure appeared in the doorway. 'Oh...' Her breath caught and fire flooded her cheeks. 'Matt...'

CHAPTER FIVE

'HELLO, Joanna.'

Joanna swallowed thickly. 'Is anything wrong?'

Matt's blue gaze scorched across her face. 'I expected to hear from you today.' Folding his arms, he leaned back against the bench of cupboards. 'And might I ask what happened to you this afternoon, sunshine?' He homed in pointedly on Jason, standing protectively at Joanna's side. 'You didn't turn up for training.'

'I didn't feel like it,' Jason said with elaborate disdain.

'Not good enough.' Matt gave a slightly grim smile. 'Even with all your ability, erratic attendance won't guarantee you a place in the team.'

'Go to hell!' the boy blazed. There was a deathly hush before Jason spun on his heel and went charging blindly from the room.

Watching her son's exit, Joanna's blood ran cold, shock draining the colour from her cheeks. 'I'm so sorry,' she said hoarsely, hugging her arms around her midriff, almost as if she were breaking in two. 'That's so out of character for Jason.'

'Your son was going for shock value, Joanna.' Matt's voice was carefully controlled. 'Believe me, I've been given much more explicit advice than that in my time. Don't worry about it.'

How could she not worry about it? Joanna wanted

to scream, but her throat wouldn't work, her legs moving automatically, stiffly, when Matt guided her into a chair and took the one beside her.

'Take it easy, Joanna,' he said quietly. 'None of this is your fault.'

She shook her head, shock holding her rigid. In her medical practice she'd dealt with the effects of teenagers who'd gone off the rails. Was her own son about to add to the statistics? She swallowed hard. 'Matt, perhaps you should just go…'

'In a minute.' Leaning forward, he took her hands in his and began absently chafing her knuckles. 'When Jason opened the door to me just now, I could've cut his antagonism with a knife. Mind telling me what's going on?'

Joanna bit the underside of her lip. 'It's complicated.'

'So tell me.'

She shook her head. 'Not here. Not now.'

'OK…' Giving her hands a little squeeze, he let her go. He looked broodingly at her for a moment, before he asked, 'Would you have an opportunity tomorrow when we could talk?'

She brought her head up, drawing in a long shaky breath. 'I could stretch to an hour between one and two o'clock.'

'Suits me.' He flicked up an eyebrow. 'I'll pick you up at the Strachan and bring lunch, OK? We'll find a spot down by the river.'

When Matt had gone, Joanna opened a bottle of wine, poured herself a glass and sat down at the kitchen table. What a mess! She sighed, feeling the crippling responsibility of being a sole parent gnawing relentlessly at her insides.

She'd drunk barely half a glass of wine when she resolutely got to her feet and went and tapped on Jason's bedroom door.

The door opened just a crack.

'I'd like you to give me a hand with dinner, please, Jason.'

'Has he gone?'

'If you mean Matt,' she said stiffly, 'yes. He left some time ago.'

Jason opened the door and somewhat reluctantly followed his mother into the kitchen. 'Sorry.'

'I think it's Matt you should be apologising to, don't you?' Joanna gave the steaks a quick pound and set them under the grill.

The boy had the grace to blush and look uncomfortable. 'He's got no right to come the heavy,' he defended.

'Is that what Matt was doing?' Joanna kept her cool with difficulty.

'Seems like it to me. He's not my father!'

Joanna's eyes widened in shock. Was this what it was all about? 'Matt's not trying to be your father, for heaven's sake! Your father is dead,' she said brutally.

When she thought about it later, Joanna couldn't remember how they'd got through the meal. Somehow, she'd finished cobbling together a salad to have with the steak and they'd sat in front of the television. Afterwards, Jason had washed up quietly and then excused himself to do his homework. Joanna had drunk another glass of wine and now she realised be-latedly her head was splitting.

'Oh, Jason,' she sighed, and felt her eyes filling. She scrubbed them with a tissue and then went along the hallway to the bathroom. Neither of them would sleep tonight if they left things like this, she thought, swallowing a couple of paracetamol.

And no matter what, she mustn't lose touch with her son. In a desperate attempt at reconciliation, she took matters into her own hands.

There was a strip of light showing under his bed-room door and she knocked and popped her head in. 'I dug out those photos of your dad, Jase. We could go through them if you like. Perhaps there's one or two you'd like to frame...'

Matt thought it was shaping up to be the longest eve-ning of his life.

All he wanted to do was to sit down and work out how best to handle the situation he'd somehow in-advertently created between Joanna and her son.

Instead, there was a backlog of paperwork from the clinic to sort out, another quit-smoking session to fa-cilitate and just today it seemed as though the possi-bility of anorexia with one of the young female ath-letes was about to raise its ugly head. And now Matt had to try to find a way to broach the subject with her mother.

He blew out a hard breath, tunnelling a hand through his hair in frustration. He needed a female medical practitioner on staff like yesterday.

He needed Joanna.

* * *

Next morning Joanna drove to work early, her manner purposeful, her mind full of resolve. She and Jason were almost back on track, but emotionally she felt they still had a way to go. And for some reason she felt she'd let him down. Quite how, she wasn't sure, but she'd earn his trust back if it was the last thing she did, she vowed, pushing open the door to Reception.

'Morning, Joanna.' Steffi was all smiles.

'You've had your hair cut!' Joanna plonked her case down and surveyed the new style with a satisfied grin. 'It looks gorgeous.' Steffi's longish curly mane was now cut to within an inch all over her head, delineating her elfin features and big green eyes.

'Thanks.' Steffi lifted a shoulder coyly. 'I like it, too. Di arranged for a hairdresser to come to the house last night to give Mum a trim and she offered to do mine while she was there.'

'Well, it's fabulous. And speaking of your mum, I know someone who will sit with her on a regular basis so you can get out and about a bit more.'

'Who?'

'Me.'

'You?' Steffi looked at her with astonished eyes.

'Hey, I'm quite capable, you know.'

Steffi shook her head. 'I didn't mean it like that, but you don't have the time—'

'I will have when I get myself reorganised.' Joanna held up her hand when Steffi would have protested. 'Jason and I had quite a long talk last night. I discovered he's missing involvement with his grandparents quite a bit. As you know, we moved here from Canberra.'

Steffi nodded, moving closer to prop her elbows on the counter top.

'Somehow, we found ourselves discussing how life is different for lots of people. For instance, Jason's never been able to experience what it's like to have a father around.'

'That must have been awful for you.'

'We managed,' Joanna said evenly. 'But only because we had a lot of help and support. Anyway, to cut a long story short, my son and I would like to extend our lives a bit, and if you think your mum would agree, we'd like to visit and hopefully offer one another some companionship.'

'Oh, Joanna…' Steffi's eyes filled and then overflowed, taking streaks of mascara down her cheeks. 'It's all been so hard for Mum. S-she was the local historian before her sight deteriorated. If Jason's at all interested in history, she'd have lots to tell him.' Steffi swallowed and dabbed at her eyes. 'She used to have quite an active social life as well. But all that seems a lifetime ago now. People just dropped off coming to visit and—'

'I know how it is, Stef.' Joanna patted her hand. She picked up her case again. 'Have a chat to your mum and let me know what suits, OK? And then go plan *your* social life,' she added with a grin.

Steffi made a face. 'If I had one.'

Joanna tossed her a meaningful little look. 'What's the expression? For everything there is a season? And I have a feeling yours is about to take off.' She took a step away and then turned back. 'Oh—I'm taking my full lunch-hour today. But you can get me on my mobile if there's anything that can't wait.'

*   *   *

Joanna's heart was trampolining as she left the building at one o'clock. And when she saw the grey Mercedes and Matt waiting, something seemed to melt her insides.

Matt looked up, seeing her cross the car park towards him. The hard knot of uncertainty in his gut began to tighten. She looked lovely in her navy trousers and bright red jumper, the sun catching the shine in her dark hair as it swung gently around her shoulders.

'Hello.' She drew to a rather breathless stop in front of him.

'Thank you for coming,' he said rather formally, holding the passenger door open for her and trying to keep his eyes off the smooth, pale skin that disappeared into creamy shadow under the V-neck of her jumper.

'Surely you didn't think I'd renege?'

'I gave up taking anything for granted a long time ago.'

Joanna glanced up as he settled the seat belt over her shoulder, but could glean nothing from his expression. 'Where are we going?' she asked lightly, and forced a smile.

'Down by the river.'

Well, she'd known that. Joanna gritted her teeth, wondering why she'd bothered to come at all when Matt seemed preoccupied and not all that pleased to see her. Because he asked you to, her romantic self offered smugly. And you've thought of nothing else but seeing him all morning.

'How're things with Jason?' Matt asked, as they stopped at a set of traffic lights.

'Better.' She rolled her bottom lip between her teeth. 'We had a long talk.'

'Good.'

There was a beat of silence, and as if propelled by something outside themselves they turned to each other, their eyes locking, his like blue lasers burning through to the very heart of her. Then inch by inch his head lowered and his mouth touched hers.

Soft. So soft and tender, fleeting. Then, slowly, he lifted his head and trapped her gaze again. And lingered. Until the indignant blare from the horn of the car directly behind startled them back to reality.

Matt muttered an expletive and shot the Mercedes forward and into a gap beyond the intersection.

'Looks like we have the place to ourselves.' Joanna looked around. Although the winter frosts had been heavy, there was still a sheen of greenness along the river bank. 'Just here?' She looked up as Matt brought a picnic basket and travel rug from the boot of the car.

Taking an end of the rug each, they spread it so that it was half in shade from the branches of the silver wattles that lined the river. Joanna dropped onto the rug with a sigh. 'It's a glorious spot, isn't it?'

They investigated the picnic basket together. There was chilled mineral water and luscious-looking chicken-and-salad sandwiches on thick wholemeal bread. And for afters, a smoky cheese and seaweed crackers, plus a couple of crisp red apples that were just waiting to be crunched.

Joanna's eyes widened in amazement. 'This is fantastic, Matt. And not a sign of cornflakes,' she quipped. 'Did you do it yourself?'

'Yeah, right.' His mouth pleated into a wry grin. 'Elle organised it with the local deli.' He opened the mineral water and filled two paper cups. 'I'm afraid I'm inclined to ask her to do quite a lot more than her job description outlines. Don't know where I could get some pleasant, intelligent office help, do you?'

Joanna shrugged. 'Not offhand. Now, shall we make a start on this delicious food?' She looked up into those blue, blue eyes. 'Hungry?'

Oh, yes, he was hungry all right. Hungry for the body of a woman. A woman to love and cherish. A woman who was special, caring. Lovely. And Joanna Winters seemed to fit the bill on all counts. He drew in a steadying breath, one that took in her delicate fragrance…

'Joanna?'

'Mmm?' She looked up from placing food on the disposable picnic plates.

'Nothing, really…' Wimp. He swallowed the gravel in his throat. 'Let's eat.'

They were both ravenous and the food disappeared at an alarming rate. When they were replete, Matt got to his feet and ambled back to the car. When he returned, he was brandishing a flask and two mugs.

'Show-off!' Joanna wrinkled her nose at him.

He made himself comfortable again on the rug. 'I take it you're passing on the coffee, then, Dr Winters?' He uncorked the flask and poured a mug of the steaming, aromatic brew and waved it under her nose.

'Don't be mean.' She pouted prettily. 'It smells divine and you've thought of everything. I can't remember the last time I—' She stopped and dipped her head defensively. 'Well, anyway, it's been lovely.'

'For me, too,' Matt rejoined quietly.

Later, Joanna couldn't have said how they'd ended up lying side by side on the rug. Perhaps it had been the crispness of a clear winter's day, the drowsing sun or the insistent drumming of the cicadas lulling them into a dreamy forgetfulness.

Matt had undone the top three buttons on his shirt and she had to suck in a lungful of air to steady herself, curling her fingers into fists to keep them from travelling over that smooth olive skin...

'You don't have to be back yet, do you?' He turned his head slowly towards her and for an instant she fancied something burned like a naked flame in the depths of his eyes.

She swallowed dryly. 'I have a little while yet.'

'Then let's relax for a few minutes, shall we?' His voice was soft, little more than a whisper, and in an almost seamless movement he folded her into his arms and lowered his mouth to hers.

At the touch of his lips, Joanna felt her body spasm, as if already he had secret access to her strings. Her nerve-ends curled and relaxed and curled again, her arms coming up to twine around his neck, holding him against her. Suddenly, as if their bodies were calling to each other, they were locked intimately together and she was clinging to him and letting him touch her at will, until she forgot to think, forgot to reason...

After an age, they pulled back and looked at each other, their breathing hard.

'Joanna…' he whispered huskily.

She lifted her hand to touch his face and found her fingers trembling. 'Matthew,' she said, and smiled tentatively.

'I don't want to let you out of my sight.' He stroked her cheek with the back of his hand. 'Come and work at the sports clinic.'

Her chest lifted in a little bubble of laughter. 'Is this how you conduct all your job interviews, Dr McKellar?'

He said nothing, just turned her into his arms and cradled her head against his shoulder. 'Does Jason resent me seeing you?' he asked after a while.

'Seems to,' she said slowly. 'He thinks you're trying to be his father.'

'What?' Matt thrust up his forearm to cover his eyes, as if to block out the impact of her words. 'For heaven's sake!'

She let out a shaky sigh. 'That was my reaction. We're halfway to being friends again but if I come to work at the clinic—'

'That's blackmail,' he growled. 'Selfish young idiot.'

His criticism of her son momentarily rankled. 'You have to remember Jason and I have been a unit for the whole of his life. And now at the impressionable age he is, it's only natural he perceives himself as the man of the family.'

Matt turned abruptly and snagged her chin, tipping her head so she had to look at him. 'And when he's grown and gone, Joanna, what then?'

She'd be on her own, she supposed. And put like that, it sounded awful.

'Would you like the job?'

She chewed her lip, still torn. 'I'm probably ready for a new challenge. I'm thirty-five. I can't imagine I'll want to be a GP for another twenty or so years.'

'Then don't be.' Matt was firm. 'Let me speak to Jason.'

'No.' Joanna shook her head. 'He'll come round. I don't want to rock the boat just yet. How long have I got?'

'A couple of days at most. The board's getting restless. They'll want to advertise by the end of the week.'

As it turned out, her decision whether or not to accept Matt's job offer was brought into sharp focus and hurried along when she arrived back at the surgery. Joanna could see Steffi was looking agitated. 'What's up?'

'Dr Strachan wants to see you.'

Joanna glanced at her watch. Mitchell Strachan was the senior partner and founder of the practice, owning the actual building in which they all worked. And she was back five minutes late, but surely—

'He's seeing everyone.' Steffi's mouth flattened in a grimace. 'Including little old me.'

Joanna felt a slick of unease. 'Am I to go in now?'

Steffi grabbed the phone as it rang beside her. 'As soon as you got back, he said.'

'OK, I'll, um, go along to his room now.' For some reason Joanna felt her breathing become immediately tight.

Twenty minutes later, she was punching out the number to Matt's direct line. It was Elle who answered.

Slightly thrown, Joanna stumbled, 'Ah…it's Joanna Winters. I must speak to Matt.'

'He's with a client,' Elle said coolly. 'May I take a message?'

Frustratedly, Joanna scooped a hand through her hair, locking her fingers in the silky fall. 'Just ask him to call me, please. As soon as he's free,' she added for good measure.

When Matt returned her call, she was with a patient and had to curtail him. 'I'll have to get back to you, Dr McKellar,' she said in professional tones for the benefit of her patient, and heard his muttered expletive. 'Ten minutes?' she enquired blandly. 'Thank you.'

Oh, those slow, ticking minutes.

One eye on the time, Joanna hastily reassured her patient, the garrulous Mrs Burns, that, no, castor oil was not an appropriate treatment for shingles.

'But I heard if I rubbed it on, Doctor—'

'There's an antiviral medication on the market now, Mrs B.,' Joanna broke in briskly. 'And as we've caught you in time, it should give you great relief from the irritation almost immediately.' Hastily, Joanna wrote out the script and handed it over. 'While you're at the chemist, ask for a non-alkaline cleanser as well. It's not a good idea to use soap at the moment.'

Joanna had barely closed the door after her patient when her phone rang. 'Matt?'

'What the hell's going on?'

Joanna took a quick breath. 'I was going to call you—'

'Never mind all that,' He overrode her with an urgent edge to his voice. 'What's up?'

Joanna plonked herself on the edge of the desk and stared blankly at the pale blue Venetian blind at her window. She could still hardly take it in...

'We're being taken over. Dr Strachan's sold the practice to one of those multinational conglomerates. They'll come in and gut the place, treble the number of doctors to generate more income for the shareholders and give us all a cubbyhole to work in. I'd have to reapply for my own job.'

'So when are you coming to me?'

'Matt...' Joanna gave a little groan. Things were moving at the speed of light. She didn't know whether she could keep up.

'You *are* going to take up my job offer, aren't you?'

Her fingers squeezed tight across her temple. She must be, mustn't she, otherwise, why had she flown to tell him what had happened? 'Yes,' she said, and then added, 'Yes,' a bit more firmly. 'The alterations are to begin almost at once so, unless I want to stay here, I don't have to hang about.' She swallowed and took the flying jump from the cliff top. 'I could start on Monday.'

'Good.' Matt sounded suddenly businesslike. 'I'll get weaving on your paperwork. And, Joanna?' His voice softened to huskiness.

Her heart fluttered. 'Yes?'

'Welcome aboard.'

Jason took the news better than Joanna had feared. They were in the kitchen when she told him.

'Why would Dr Strachan want to sell to those morons?' he snorted, pulling the ring top on a can of soft drink.

'Because he's getting on in years, I suppose.' Joanna strove to be fair, spooning instant coffee into a mug. 'And probably because he saw it as an opportunity to get a lump sum together for his retirement. And he might not have had the chance again. The people who orchestrate these kinds of takeovers don't hesitate to move on if people start dithering about whether to sell or not.'

'What about your patients?'

Joanna sighed. That part was killing her. 'I've already begun contacting them and telling them what's happening. I imagine most of them will continue to come to the clinic and take their chance with a new doctor.'

Jason fiddled with the knot in his school tie. 'So— are you going to take the job at the sports-medicine clinic?'

'I've told Matt I would. I need the challenge, Jase,' she added after a long pause, knowing she sounded almost pleading, but he hadn't said anything, just stood against the doorframe, taking mouthfuls of his drink.

'I'm pulling out of the basketball team, Mum.'

'Why?' As if she didn't know.

Jason reddened slightly. 'It's not what you think,' he said defensively. 'I just want to concentrate on my athletics. I'm in the hundred metres sprint and long jump. I should do OK, don't you reckon?'

Joanna looked up and sent him a crooked smile. 'Well you've certainly got the legs for it.' Opening the fridge, she took out milk for her coffee. 'Will you tell Matt, then?' she asked casually, and sensed her son's almost palpable unease.

'I thought you might.'

'Wouldn't it be the mature thing for *you* to tell him?'

Jason's eyes filled with uncertainty.

Almost holding her breath, Joanna watched her son's throat tighten with heartbreaking vulnerability. Was she pushing him too far?

He crunched his empty can and tossed it into the bin. 'I guess I could swing by the club after school tomorrow…'

'That might be a good idea.' Joanna nodded, relief flooding through her. Given all the circumstances, it was a daunting prospect for an adolescent to face up to. She was so proud of him. And she was sure Matt would meet him halfway. But, oh, lord, why was bringing up kids such a minefield?

'With your new job…' Jason was suddenly light-hearted, dragging off his tie and tossing it over the back of a chair '…we'll still be able to go and see Steffi's mum, won't we?'

'Of course. Absolutely.'

'Cool.' Jason's face was wreathed in smiles. ''Cos there's a comp for a history essay about the early days of Glenville coming up. The first prize is a weekend trip to the Sydney museum. I thought Mrs Phillips might be able to clue me in and I could write stuff the other guys won't have.'

'Well, then…' Joanna flicked out a hand and ruffled his hair. 'We'd better see what we can arrange. Hadn't we?'

CHAPTER SIX

'SORRY to throw you in at the deep end,' Matt apologised on Monday morning.

Joanna touched the neckline of her brand-new T-shirt with the clinic's logo and yanked in a breath to still her nerves. It was all so different. 'What do you have for me?'

'A possible case of anorexia.' He frowned at the contents of the slim file. 'I wanted to give you a slow and leisurely orientation,' he said ruefully. 'But this can't wait.'

Joanna tugged her chair closer. 'Fill me in.'

'Sasha Wardell, age fifteen.' Matt's mouth compressed. 'We've only come across her by chance. Her mother brought her here for some physio after a back injury. Elle expressed her concerns to me after she'd treated the girl initially.'

Joanna's eyes widened in query. 'What kind of activity is she into that would cause the injury?'

'She's a gymnast. Very promising, from all accounts. She's aiming for the Olympics.'

'And starving herself in the process, by the sound of it.' Joanna took the file and ran through the scant information. 'Obviously we have to tread carefully and if she's in denial, it's going to be a long haul.'

'And best handled by my new associate.'

Joanna sent him a sugary smile. 'You've been saving this up for me, haven't you?'

'Not true.' Matt palmed his innocence. 'Sasha only came to us a few days ago. I was still considering the best way to go.'

'Hmm.' Joanna closed the file, two tiny earnest lines jumping into sharp relief between her brows. 'As a priority, I'd like to talk to the mother. Sasha's a juvenile. I can't start treating her without parental permission. But obviously I'll need to observe the youngster beforehand.' She looked preoccupied, her mind focused on the best possible path to take. 'Any chance I could look in on one of her physio sessions?'

'As a matter of fact, she's with Elle now.' Matt leaned forward and his knuckles brushed her cheek briefly. 'I'll take you down.'

'It's possible the mother has concerns too, and is finding it difficult to voice them,' Joanna said consideringly as they made their way down the stairs from Matt's office and onto a mezzanine floor.

'Very possible,' he agreed, pushing back a curtain and leading her between a series of couches and pieces of rehab equipment. 'You'll find Elle in the screened-off cube in the corner.'

'Right.' Joanna nodded. 'I'll keep it all low-key.'

'And check back with me.' Matt touched her fleetingly on the shoulder.

Joanna pulled aside the cheerful floral curtain around the cubicle and stepped inside. 'Good morning, Elle.'

'Doctor,' the physio acknowledged stiffly.

Joanna sighed inwardly. She'd have to try to find a way to break down Elle's antagonism. It didn't need rocket science to work out the physio considered Matt her private property. That she resented Joanna coming on staff had been apparent from her frosty little reception earlier in his office. 'OK if I look in on your session for a minute?'

'Be my guest.'

Joanna shrugged off the less than gracious invitation. In the rough and tumble of medical training, she'd come up against the odd difficult personality. In the larger scheme of things, one more was neither here or there. Instead, she switched her mind to what she was here for and sent their young patient a warm smile. 'Hi, Sasha. I'm Joanna. How's it going?'

In baggy shorts and T-shirt, Sasha was lying on her back, looking wide-eyed and vulnerable. 'Still hurts a bit.'

'Try the hamstring stretches for me now, please, Sasha,' Elle came in with brisk authority. 'Position your hands behind your thigh to support your leg and pull up. Straighten your leg, honey. That's it. Hold for twenty and come down slowly. Good work. Couple more of those and then we'll get some heat onto that muscle. Are you getting out of bed the way I showed you?'

'Rolling onto my side and pushing up through my arms.' The youngster turned a hopeful smile in Elle's direction. 'Are you going to give me a massage today?'

'You bet.' Elle busied herself with the small trolley that held the apparatus for transferring the heat probes to the injured muscles. 'Like some music as well?'

'Yes, please.'

Even that short workout had the child looking exhausted. Joanna slid her hands into the side pockets of her trousers, nibbling her lip in conjecture. Sasha was certainly very thin, almost to the point of fragility, and her skin was exceptionally pale. Perhaps she never saw the sun. And if that was the case, they could be looking at a vitamin D deficiency as well.

'Thank you, Elle.' Joanna looked purposeful as she turned and slipped from the cubicle. Sasha Wardell's health needed further investigation. And urgently.

Bent on her mission, she went in search of Matt.

'You're seriously worried, aren't you?' Leading the way back to his office, he pushed her gently into a chair. 'Coffee-time.'

Joanna rested her chin on her hand, watching him. 'Is there a chance Sasha's mother will be coming to collect her?'

'That's been the m.o., I believe.' Matt placed the mug of coffee in front of her and sent her a crooked smile. 'No doughnuts, I'm afraid.'

'Bad for the hips.' Joanna lifted the hot drink and sipped gratefully. 'From what I observed, and my limited knowledge of physio procedures, I'd say Elle will be about another half-hour with Sasha. In the meantime, I could probably slip in a quick consult with the mum and then, guided by what she can tell me, I'll talk to Sasha.'

'Sounds good.' Matt glanced at his watch. 'If your timing's right, Mrs Wardell should be here directly. She usually waits in the foyer until Sasha's finished.'

'OK.' Joanna gulped down the rest of her coffee and got to her feet.

Matt put out a restraining hand. 'Tell me exactly how you're going to play this.'

She blinked. Was he about to put a brake on her autonomy? Well, she wasn't having that. Either she worked on equal terms with him or not at all. She managed a stiff kind of smile which didn't quite reach her eyes. 'Don't you trust me to handle matters my own way?'

'Until your orientation is complete, I need to keep an eye on things.'

'Don't you mean keep an eye on me?' She brought her chin up, refusing to flinch.

'No, I don't.' He scrubbed a hand across his cheekbones in obvious frustration. 'Joanna, I'm the director here. That means I'm responsible for the kind of care and advice our clients are given.'

Joanna huffed her distaste. 'So, they're *clients* we deal with here, are they? Not patients!' She turned away, her expression tight. 'You should've told me, Matthew.'

'Joanna…' Matt reached for, hauling her in against him and forcing her to acknowledge him. 'Stop it,' he cajoled softly. 'You'll be brilliant.'

'Will I?' Disturbed by the sensations he was arousing, she braced her palms against his chest and tilted herself back.

Matt's dry smile pleated the corners of his mouth. 'I have every faith in you, Dr Winters.'

'Well, that's a relief.' She gave a shaky smile. 'You'll have to excuse my first-day nerves. And it has been a stressful few days—leaving the Strachan and everything…'

'I know.' Matt put his hands to her elbows, smoothing them up inside the sleeves of her T-shirt to enclose her upper arms. 'And I'm sorry if I've seemed to add to your sense of feeling pressured.' His blue eyes glinted with dry humour. 'But I had to get you here somehow, didn't I?'

His look was so intense, her heart leapt, banging a drumbeat inside her chest, and she had to step back, breaking his hold on her arms. 'Did…Jason come to see you?' she sidetracked quickly, looking at the floor. 'He hasn't said anything and I haven't liked to ask.'

A beat of silence.

'Yes, he did. We talked man to man.'

Joanna looked up quickly, glimpsing something measured in the blue depths of his eyes. She swallowed. 'And?'

He lifted a shoulder. 'I don't think he hates my guts quite as much as he thought he did, but he's certainly protective of you, Joanna.' His smile was a twisted parody. 'I'll have to watch where I put my size nines in future.'

She made a sound in protest. 'It's not a contest, Matt.'

'I'm aware of that,' he said bluntly. 'But if it were, I have to wonder which way you'd choose, Joanna.'

Her throat dried and her voice came out a bit cracked. 'That isn't fair. And it certainly isn't the time or place for this conversation.'

'You brought it up.'

She licked her lips. 'Be sure I won't make the same mistake again.' She moved purposefully towards the door. 'Now, are *we* going to speak to Mrs Wardell?'

'You go.' Matt's mouth clamped. 'You can't miss her. She's a tall, very striking blonde.'

So he'd noticed.

Ten minutes later, Joanna had her worse fears confirmed. Sasha's mother—or Gerri, as she asked to be called—had seemed desperate to talk.

'I haven't known quite where to turn,' she confessed. 'I mean, you hear and read such dreadful things about teenage girls starving themselves...'

'And you're quite sure Sasha's not getting her periods?' Wanting to keep the interview informal, Joanna wasn't taking notes, preferring to store the information away in her head.

'Quite sure.' Gerri nodded, twisting the large emerald ring on her middle finger. 'Well, as a mother, you notice those kinds of things, don't you?'

'I can't comment on that.' Joanna gave a contained little smile. 'I have a teenage son. What about Sasha's father? Does she have a good relationship with him?'

The mother's face looked suddenly pinched. 'We're divorced. He's remarried. Lives in Sydney now. Sasha gets to see him only during school holidays.' She looked down at her hands for a moment. 'And it's difficult for her—with the new wife and everything.'

So, lots going on for a young person to cope with. Joanna thought quickly, running through the classic signs of anorexia in her mind. 'You understand, Mrs Wardell—Gerri—that if we're going to treat Sasha, we'll need to tread very carefully.'

'You *are* going to treat my daughter, then?' The mother's relief was palpable.

'If you give us permission to.'

'Oh, yes! Yes—please. My child needs help, Dr Winters. And another thing...' Suddenly the information began tumbling out. 'When I've been cleaning the bath lately, I've been finding handfuls of hair caught in the plughole. Could that be related to...?' She stopped and swallowed.

'Very probably,' Joanna responded gently. 'What about mood swings? I realise most adolescents have them, but are Sasha's exaggerated would you say?'

Gerri's gaze faltered before she nodded slowly. 'I've been feeling an absolute failure as a parent...' Her brown eyes suddenly filled. 'Poor little Sasha...'

Joanna found Matt in one of the examination rooms.

'Joanna.' He acknowledged her presence with a curt nod. 'Something I can do for you?'

'I need to confer with you, please.'

'Sure. This is Paul Camden, one of our ace young footballers.' Matt replaced the modesty sheet over his patient's abdomen. 'Paul, this is Joanna Winters. She's come to join our medical team.'

'Hi.' The young man sent a quick smile in Joanna's direction. Then, lifting himself up on his elbows, he turned his gaze urgently on Matt. 'So, what do you reckon, Doc?'

'We'll need to run a few tests to see what's going on but I'm reasonably certain you have a hernia in your groin.'

'Hell!' The young athlete flopped back down onto the bed. 'This is gonna put me right out of the finals, isn't it?'

'Afraid so.' Matt parked himself on the edge of the couch. 'I won't beat about the bush with you. From what I've seen today, you'll need a surgical repair.'

'Ball-park figure, how long before I can train again?'

'For soccer?' Matt rubbed a hand across his chin. 'Two to four months minimum.'

'That's what I figured.' The young man looked glum. 'Thanks anyway, Doc.' He turned his face to the wall.

'Hey, don't start jumping the gun here.' Matt pushed to his feet. 'Let's see what the herniography turns up. And then we'll discuss your options. OK? Back in a minute.'

'Let's go in here,' Matt said shortly, and Joanna accompanied him into one of the small conference rooms. He folded his arms and leaned back against the wall. 'I take it this is about Sasha?'

'I have Mrs Wardell's permission for us to treat her. She's seriously worried—and with reason, I think.'

'Let's go ahead, then.'

Joanna dragged in a steadying breath. 'Do you want to sit in as an observer?'

Matt's jaw clenched. 'No, I don't.'

'Oh.'

He gave a click of annoyance. 'You're not on trial here, Joanna.'

'Funny.' Her lashes flickered up. 'I thought I was.'

Matt wanted to shake her. Make love to her. And everything in between. Why had he ever thought this would work? 'What have you done with Mrs Wardell?'

'Sent her off uptown for a coffee.' Joanna ignored his dark look. 'I've told her to come back in an hour.'

'I'll leave things in your capable hands, then,' he said, his voice clipped and impersonal. 'Now, if there's nothing else, I'll get back to my client.' He pushed himself away from the wall and reached for the doorhandle. 'Brief me later, please.'

Watching him walk away, Joanna felt her spirits sink to the floor. His back was forbiddingly straight, leaving no doubt that on a personal level he was shutting her out.

Oh, Matt.

She blinked the sudden dampness away from her eyes. She wouldn't play these games. Couldn't. Suddenly, she felt about a hundred years old.

She gave herself a mental shake. For heaven's sake! She wasn't about to cave in on her first day. She couldn't afford to anyway, she thought dryly. She had to keep this job no matter how tough it got. She had a growing son to feed and clothe. Hauling in a long, calming breath, she made her way back to the physio department.

Elle was just tidying up after her session with Sasha. 'Hi.' She greeted Joanna and actually managed a brief smile.

'I'm looking for Sasha.' Joanna looked quickly around. Surely the child hadn't gone!

'She's in the loo.' Elle threw several towels into a waiting receptacle. 'I've told her we need a medical profile and that you might want a word. Well, Matt said you probably would.' She added the rider with a little shrug.

'Well spotted, by the way.' Joanna sent out the warmest vibrations she could muster, not really expecting the other woman to respond.

But Elle did. Her teeth caught on her bottom lip as she looked down at the bundle of linen she'd stripped off the couch. 'I hope you can help her, Joanna. She's a really sweet kid.'

Joanna drew confidingly closer. 'Hadn't her coach noticed anything?'

Elle shook her head. 'Adolescents are pretty good at camouflage.'

And not only adolescents, Joanna thought darkly. Adults made a pretty good job of it as well.

'You could talk to Sasha in my office, if you like.' Elle seemed to be going out of her way to be helpful. 'It's a pretty non-threatening environment and everything's there that you'll need.' She twitched a shoulder. 'I know you won't have had time to get your own domain set up yet.'

'Thank you.' Joanna drummed up a warm smile. 'That's very generous of you.'

'Matt's aim here is to promote a harmonious workplace.' Elle tucked a frond of hair behind her ear. 'I'd like to think it could continue.'

Joanna took in a long breath and let it go. 'Well, that's certainly put me on my mettle,' she murmured, her eyes narrowing on the physio's long easy stride towards another curtained-off cubicle and another of her clients.

Joanna recorded Sasha's blood pressure, not surprised at the low reading. Equally worrying, her pulse at ninety was very fast, indicating dehydration and malnutrition. Joanna's medical antennae were immediately on alert.

But softly, softly, she cautioned herself. First she would have to get Sasha's trust, and then and only then could they work towards a successful outcome.

'When did you last eat, Sasha?'

'Breakfast.' Almost defensively, the fifteen-year-old clutched her little bright red bucket bag to her chest.

'Mind telling me what you had?'

Sasha twitched a thin shoulder. 'The usual stuff.'

'I see.' Joanna kept her voice pitched to a warm neutrality. 'Fruit, cereal, toast? Any of those?'

The girl's throat moved convulsively as she swallowed. 'Some fruit, I think.'

'What was it?' Joanna asked carefully.

'Can't remember.'

No joy there. After the tiniest pause, Joanna smiled and drew back into the softness of the leather chair. 'So, Sasha, how long have you been doing gymnastics?'

The youngster's face brightened at the change of subject. 'My dad took me to classes when I was seven. He was a brilliant gymnast. He trained under the Russian coach, Serge Mishcof,' she added proudly.

It could have been under Mickey Mouse and Joanna would have been no more enlightened. Nevertheless, she strove to look impressed. 'Did he get to any of the big games?'

The girl shook her head. 'He had to give up when he was nineteen. He got too heavy...'

Joanna's intuition sharpened. Was the child trying to take over where her father had had to leave off? It could be as simple as that. Or as complicated, she warned herself silently.

On the other hand, as Sasha's doctor now, she had to make a snap decision. There wasn't time to second guess if they were to avoid a crisis with the youngster's health. If they didn't act now, her young life could very well go down the plughole, along with her baby-blonde hair.

Joanna switched back into professional mode. 'I'd like to take some blood from you now, if that's OK.'

'Why?'

'Just as a precaution.' Joanna wound the cuff around Sasha's thin upper arm. 'You appear quite a bit underweight for your height. Flex your fingers for me now, please, so I can tap a vein.' It was a struggle but Joanna finally got enough blood sample to be sent off for testing. If the result didn't come back showing Sasha's iron stores were drastically low, she'd take her medical-degree certificate out of its frame and eat it.

'How are your periods, Sasha?' Joanna secured the vial and labelled it.

Silence.

Then, slowly and almost too low for Joanna to hear, she mumbled, 'I...haven't had them for ages...' She raised stricken eyes. 'Are you going to tell my mum?'

Joanna leaned forward and took the youngster's slender wrist. 'She knows already, Sasha. And thank you for being honest with me. I know it took a lot of courage.'

'Am I in big tr-trouble?' The child began to blink rapidly.

'Not so big we can't find a way out of it.' Joanna squeezed and then let go. Standing, she went to the cooler and got them both a glass of water. 'Mind telling me why you're not eating?'

After the longest pause, the youngster lifted her glass and took an agonisingly slow mouthful of water, swallowing it as though it hurt her throat. 'The other gymnasts are younger—and skinnier.' Her teeth came down to clench on her bottom lip. 'If I put on weight, I'll get chucked out of the elite squad. I want to get to the Athens Games. Dad could come and watch me and—'

'Be proud of you,' Joanna finished quietly.

Eventually, Sasha nodded.

Joanna felt a cold river of warning run up her spine. They were swimming in very deep waters here. It was obvious Sasha had unresolved feelings about her father leaving the family and her parents' subsequent divorce. Did she see herself responsible in some way and was she perhaps seeking a way to win back his approval through her sport?

Whatever the reason, the child needed skilled counselling and that was right out of Joanna's territory. But first and foremost was Sasha's physical health and well-being and that, Joanna knew she could handle.

'Right, Sasha,' she said briskly, pulling a scribble pad towards her. 'You've been honest with me so I'll be honest with you. Healthwise, you'll be in serious trouble if you don't change your lifestyle. Because you've been starving yourself, your whole system's out of whack. Your body is like a delicately balanced machine—you have to take care of it if you want it to work properly. That sounds reasonable, doesn't it?'

'I guess…'

'Now, as a priority,' Joanna continued, 'I want you and your mum to talk to one of our dieticians here.

For starters, you need to begin eating meat—or pasta if you prefer—lots of fresh fruit and veg and high-energy protein-supplement drinks.'

Sasha's pretty mouth flattened in resignation. 'What if I get too heavy for my routine on the parallel bars?'

'Initially it might be disappointing but it won't be the end of your life. The main thing is you'll be fit and healthy again.'

Sasha seemed unconvinced.

'Talk to Dr McKellar or one of the coaches here.' Joanna spread her hands in a philosophical gesture. 'Even if your bone and muscle mass increase to an extent you aren't suited to gymnastics, there must be a dozen other sports disciplines you could excel at.'

A tiny dimple flickered in Sasha's cheek. 'Like sumo wrestling?'

Joanna's snip of laughter was spontaneous. She wanted to hug the child for rising so quickly to the surface, after nearly drowning.

Good for you, sweetheart, she thought in admiration. If the youngster could keep her sense of humour to that extent, she was already halfway to recovery.

Joanna could hardly believe it was almost lunchtime. The morning had simply flown. In their initial meeting that morning, Matt had told her to take a break whenever she needed it. There were no hard and fast rules.

Oh, help. She placed a hand hastily on her tummy as it grumbled. She'd better eat sooner rather than later.

The staffroom was deserted. Joanna didn't know

whether to be disappointed or glad. On one hand she wanted to be quiet, on the other she was dying to unload the details of her morning so far with Matt. As if her thoughts had conjured him up, he stuck his head around the door.

'Oh, good. You're here. Mind if I join you?'

'Of course not.' Joanna managed a tentative smile. Going to the fridge, she took out the salad she'd brought for her lunch and then moved to plug in the electric kettle. 'Can I get you a coffee?'

'Ah, no, thanks.' He peered in the fridge and pulled out a carton of chocolate-flavoured milk. 'Energy hit.' He tossed her a wry grin, before ripping the carton open. He took up his stance by the window. 'How's your morning been?'

'Very full on.' Joanna ran her eye over the selection of herbal teas and chose a peppermint.

His head came round, the light from the window illuminating the hard line of his jaw. 'Is this a good time for debriefing?'

Joanna left her teabag to infuse. 'Are we likely to be interrupted?'

Matt glanced at his watch. 'Possibly. My office, then?'

'Fine.' Joanna picked up her tea-mug and plastic lunchbox and followed him.

It was almost *déjà vu*, she thought. They were sitting at the window as they'd done on that first morning they'd met, when she'd come to sort out the nude calendar business. And so much had happened since then...

'Why the big sigh?'

Joanna looked uncertainly at him. 'Nothing.' She

aimed her salad fork at his carton of milk. 'Is that all you're having?' Good grief, she groaned inwardly. She sounded like his wife! That thought brought a flush to her cheeks and she hastily speared a wedge of tomato and lifted it to her mouth.

'I've stopped growing.' Legs comfortably outstretched and feet crossed at the ankles, Matt studied the soft curve of her mouth, stifling the urge to whirl her up from her chair and kiss her senseless. Instead, he drew his thoughts up sharply, running a professional eye over her instead. So far today, she'd used up a large amount of nervous energy, he'd do better to let her refuel.

Joanna finished her salad, hardly tasting it. How could she, she fretted, with him sitting there? He was pretending to be engrossed in a report but Joanna knew he wasn't. The goose-bumps on her arms were telling her that!

She carefully placed the lid back on her container and pushed it to one side. 'I've had a breakthrough with Sasha.'

Matt's dark head came up and he looked at her keenly. 'You're that certain?'

'Practising as a GP gives you an instinct about these things. I don't believe Sasha is a classic anorexic.'

He merely raised an eyebrow.

'I've scheduled another appointment with Gerri Wardell tomorrow.' Joanna eyed him steadily over her mug. 'I want to allay her fears. Sasha doesn't appear to be driven by body image as such but she's certainly starving herself.'

'To what end?' Matt asked carefully.

'It's all to do with her sporting aspirations and the very fixed idea she has of being too heavy to continue in the elite squad. Apparently her father had high hopes in his youth of pursuing gymnastics but matured quite early and had to give up.'

Matt scraped his fingers around his jaw. 'So she's trying to take up where her father left off. Trying to please him in her childlike way?'

'Seems like it.' Joanna made a small face. 'There's obviously some post-divorce mopping up still to be done. Sasha's anxiety has to be addressed. I'm going to suggest family counselling as a priority—even if the child's father has to fly up from Sydney to take part.'

Matt's mouth drew in. 'That's a big call. I understand he's remarried. But, on the other hand, if his daughter's health and emotional well-being are at stake, we should do everything to encourage him to resolve things.'

Joanna felt her spirits lift, relieved he understood.

'Who did you have in mind for the sessions?' he asked, and felt her hesitation.

'I've looked over your names here but if you've no objection, I'd like to refer the family to Sally Ekersley. She's outstanding in her field, sensitive, approachable...' She broke off. 'I think she could really help this family function again, even if they have to do it apart.'

'You sound as if you've taken the Wardells to your heart,' Matt said deeply.

She brought her chin up. 'I know how to stay at a professional distance, Matt. But all the time I was treating Sasha, I couldn't help thinking it could just as easily have been Jason sitting there all screwed up and desperate.'

'I can't imagine that, Joanna.' Matt's gaze became shuttered. She was sitting so still, looking soft and so vulnerable, and with everything in him he wanted to reach for her, wrap his strength around her. But right now he wasn't certain if she'd want him to do that. Wasn't certain about her in any direction for that matter. 'Your relationship with your son is very tight.'

She glanced at him quickly. It hadn't sounded like a compliment. In fact, rather the opposite. His voice had had an edge to it and the faintest thread of—what? Bitterness? Resentment? Criticism?

'No disrespect, Matt.' Joanna chose her words carefully. 'But you've never been a parent.' She took a deep breath and let it go.

For a second Matt's eyes seemed to lose their colour, glaze and go distant. His jaw worked. Giving an almost imperceptible inclination of his head, he picked up his report again and began to turn the pages.

Watching him, feeling the atmosphere between them tightening like the strings of a violin, Joanna knew why she'd avoided getting involved with anyone for the last umpteen years. When it happened, it was like trailing through fog. Because once that person was there, a part of your life, it changed the balance of your whole world. Except Matt wasn't a part of her personal life at all. And never would be if Jason had anything say in the matter.

A tiny frown pleated her forehead. Perhaps she should have tried harder at this relationship business when Jason had been younger. If she'd found some-

one, he could have slipped more easily into their
lives, been a decent stepdad, a role model for her son.
She stopped, wearied by the futile backtracking of her
thoughts.

But they wouldn't let go.

It wasn't as though she'd sought to keep her son
entirely to herself. She *had* tried to meet people. All
right—prospective husbands, or partners as they were
called now. But she'd been much younger then and
so had the men she'd dated. There had been several
special ones—but they'd been busy with life and getting established in their chosen careers. And once
they'd realised she came with a child attached, it had
all got too difficult, too onerous. Bring up someone
else's kid? Ah, don't think I'm ready for that,
Joanna—sorry.

Her shoulders lifted in a dispirited little sigh. 'I've
left my notes on Sasha for you. They're fairly detailed
but obviously if you want to discuss anything—'

'I'm sure they'll be fine,' he broke in, his voice
professionally clipped. 'Now, I don't want to rush
you, but we've still a lot of work to get through before
we can call it a day.'

'Mind if I take a minute to freshen up?'

'Go ahead.' Matt got to his feet and pushed his
chair in. 'How do you feel about looking in on one
of our quit-smoking sessions?'

'Fine.' What else could she say? It was apparent
he wanted her there, and after all she was here to
learn.

'These are a group who decided to quit a couple
of weeks ago,' Matt said, as they left the office and
began walking down the stairs. 'We'll chat to them

informally both as a group and individually. See what progress they've made and how they're feeling about things generally.'

'Sounds interesting.' Joanna's enthusiasm was a trifle forced and her smile didn't quite reach her eyes.

CHAPTER SEVEN

IT WAS so good to be home.

Joanna nosed her car into the garage and cut the engine. Blocking a yawn, she raised her arms to shoulder height, stretching to relieve the ache in her neck and the small of her back.

After a few seconds, she lowered her arms, fumbling across to the passenger seat to retrieve her shoulder bag, decrying the fact she had hardly enough energy to do even that, let alone get out of the car.

In fact, she thought wryly, if it wasn't so cramped, she'd have been tempted to put her head down on the steering-wheel and drop off. But then she really *would* have had a stiff neck in the morning. Her breath came out in a ragged sigh as she pushed herself out of the car, rocking to her feet a bit unsteadily.

'I didn't think you'd be *this* late! I've been hanging about for ages!'

The sight of her son, arms folded, feet planted aggressively apart and towering over her, snapped Joanna's fragile control. 'Stop sounding like my father, Jason!' Tossing her bunch of keys to him, she added tetchily, 'If you want to be helpful, bring my case in.'

As he'd done dozens of times, Jason brought her medical case in and carefully placed it the hall cupboard. Then, walking soft-footed in his trainers, he came back into the lounge where Joanna sat on the sofa, head lowered, her fingers gently massaging her temples. He ground his bottom lip uncertainly, rocking a bit awkwardly on the balls of his feet. 'Would you, uh, like a glass of wine?'

Joanna shook her head. Her nerves were stretched and she was almost brain-dead with fatigue, but she'd hadn't meant to be so impatient with her son. 'No, thanks, love.'

'What are we doing for dinner?'

Joanna groaned inwardly. Teenage boys. Why did their minds continually focus on food and more food? She brought her head up, the corners of her mouth pleating in a trapped smile. 'There's a pasta bake in the freezer. We could reheat it in the microwave and make a green salad to go with it.'

'Or we could dial up a pizza.' Jason gave her a tentative, hopeful grin.

Joanna palmed her hands in a capitulating shrug. 'Why not?'

Jason gave a whoop of triumph. 'What kind do you want, Mum?' He already had the cordless phone to his ear.

'You choose.' Joanna flapped a hand in his general direction and rose to her feet. 'I'm going to hit the shower.'

The pizza arrived, de-luxe size and groaning with every topping imaginable. And Joanna was feeling halfway to being human again. Revived from the shower and lashings of her favourite gel, she'd dressed for comfort in a well-worn tracksuit, shoving her feet into a pair of Jason's football socks. 'Mmm, that smells delicious.' She lifted her nose and breathed in appreciatively as Jason peeled back the cardboard lid with a flourish. 'I might have a glass of wine after all. Want a cola?' she tossed back over her shoulder, on her way to the fridge.

'Yep—please. Can we eat in front of the telly?'

'What's on?'

'One of our favourites.'

'Hmm. OK, then.'

The show eventually came to an end and the credits ran up the screen. 'Anything else you want to watch?' Jason sprawled on the carpet, his weight balanced easily on one elbow, a hip and a muscular length of leg.

Joanna shook her head. 'Don't think so.' Perhaps she'd catch a late news bulletin before she went to bed. Bending forward, she ran a finger playfully up the back of her son's neck. 'Sorry I was a bit ratty earlier, Jase.'

'No big deal.' Jason's quick turn of his head was accompanied by a forgiving grin. 'Was it a rough day?'

'Kind of, I suppose.' Joanna said slowly, thinking about it.

In one swift movement, he swivelled to face her, bringing his knees up to his chin and wrapping his arms around his shins. He was frowning heavily. 'I thought you said this job would give you more time to yourself.'

'It will eventually.' She fiddled with the metal tag on her track-top zipper. 'But initially, as well as practising, I have to learn and absorb how things are done. It's a bit like when you began your first year at high school. There's a lot to get your head around. But once I have the hang of things, I'll more or less be able to work my own hours.'

'Are you going to like working with—with Matt?'

A whole slather of butterflies ran riot in Joanna's stomach. Oh, lord, she thought. Ask me in three months' time. 'I can't see why not,' she prevaricated instead. 'How's school?' She switched lanes quickly.

'Coach reckons I'm in with a good chance to take the hundred metres at the inter-schools' track meet.' Jason was grinning from ear to ear.

'Don't get too cocky now,' Joanna warned. 'It's big-league stuff we're talking about here, isn't it?'

'Pretty big.' Jason looked down at his feet, a lock of hair flipping down on his forehead. 'If I win, I get to go the State finals and then to the Nationals—'

'Whoa, there!' Joanna's voice was more curt than she'd intended, and Jason sent her a questioning look. Suddenly restless, she swung her feet to the floor and sat watching him. She just hoped her son wasn't setting himself up to take a huge disappointment if he was beaten for first place. Perhaps she could get Matt to talk to him. She stopped, her heart twisting painfully. Perhaps nothing. At the moment, she felt she couldn't ask Matt for anything. She scraped up a smile. 'Your dad always said everything depended on how you performed on the day.'

'Yeah, but if I'm fit and I've trained properly, I'll walk it.'

Brash, youthful confidence, Joanna thought, getting to her feet. 'When is it again?' She bent to gather up the empty pizza box and the crumple of paper servi-ettes.

'Six weeks from last Friday.' In one co-ordinated movement, Jason sprang upright. 'Will you be there?'

Joanna ran through the time span in her head. By then she should have her workload organised. 'Wouldn't miss it.' She smiled. Carrying the stuff for the bin, she went through to the kitchen.

'Ah…Mum?' Jason loped after her. 'Steffi rang. Can we sit with her mum on Saturday night? I said yes but that you'd probably ring her back.'

In a second Joanna's hopes for a quiet weekend to recoup her energies nosedived. But she'd offered, hadn't she? Insisted, really. 'Of course we can. I'll give her a call later. Now, you…' She made a shooing motion with her hand. 'Homework, please.'

'Yeah, yeah,' Jason sang, sauntering off to his bedroom, seemingly quite happy to be chivvied along.

Joanna put the kettle on for coffee and then stepped outside onto the back deck. She lent on the railings, looking out. It was a beautiful night, clear and winter-crisp. Tilting her gaze, she looked skywards to where a sliver of moon and necklace of stars looked close enough to touch.

Recent memories came flooding back. Of the time she'd gone to Featherdale with Matt. It had been a lovely night then, too, with the sprays of moonlight filtering through the trees, the magical glow of the camp fire and the soft plucking of the guitarist to accompany his love song.

Even now, Joanna could feel the pressure of Matt's hand as they'd listened, hear the words of the song in her head…

Her eyes filled and overflowed and she lifted her hands and scrubbed at the tears with the heels of her hands. If Scott hadn't been injured, would she and Matt have become lovers that night? Would they have come together, clung together, drowning in deep, hungry kisses…?

Imagining it, she fantasised, moistening her lips, feeling the pleasurable ache at the feminine core of her body.

It was several moments before she registered the insistent ringing of the telephone. Hastily, she pressed the tips of her fingers to her cheeks as if to rearrange her muscles and hurried inside.

Hearing the phone ring, Jason had come bounding from his room but stopped short at the doorway, seeing his mother had the call covered.

Joanna had stepped back into the kitchen, blinking at the sudden glare of light. Suddenly all thumbs, a bit disorientated, she picked up the receiver. 'Joanna Winters.'

'Joanna, it's me.'

'Matt…' Her pulse began to race. Was it too wild to think he'd been looking at the moon and stars like her, fantasising like her? 'How lovely to hear your voice.' The words spilled out.

'You heard it only a couple of hours ago.' His short laugh was gruff but she could tell he was pleased. 'I've just picked up a flyer from the library,' he continued. 'The Sydney Symphony Orchestra's playing Beethoven's Ninth at the town hall on Saturday evening. I, uh, wondered if you'd like to go with me?'

'Oh, Matt, I'd love to—'

As she'd said it Matt cut in, responding with a light-hearted rush, 'Terrific! Perhaps we could grab a late supper afterwards—or come back to my place?'

'Matt…' Joanna felt as though a giant hand were twisting her heart. 'You didn't let me finish. I *would* love to go but Jason and I have already made plans. I'm sorry…'

It seemed an eternity before he spoke but she could imagine what he must be thinking—that she'd put Jason before him again. Spanning her fingertips across her forehead, she tried to salvage something, perhaps a shred of his pride. 'Are they playing only the one performance?'

'Ah, yes. But, look, it's not a problem.'

Well, to Joanna it was. She felt terrible, as though she'd thrown stones at him from a great height, wounding him. 'Matt…' Her heart squeezed tighter. 'We could still do something some time. Ask me again.'

'Like in about another five years.' His voice had a hollow ring. 'I'll see you tomorrow, Joanna.' He rang off quietly.

Jason had listened unashamedly from the doorway. Watching his mother replace the handset, he asked quietly, 'Was that Matt?'

She looked up at him, her head jerking in a bleak little nod. 'He invited me a concert on Saturday night.'

'But we're going to Steffi's, aren't we?' he insisted, ducking his head as if he couldn't meet her eyes.

'Yes, we are,' Joanna said, and her voice sounded rusty and unused. 'Don't worry, you'll get your research from Mrs Phillips. Perhaps it might be an idea to take your tape recorder as well.'

*   *   *

Joanna drove to work the next morning wondering how on earth she was going to cope. A strained atmosphere between Matt and herself wasn't going to be conducive to the harmony he was so insistent on.

Perhaps she should get out now, before he got any further with her orientation. He could find another female doctor to fill her place—one who didn't come with baggage.

She parked her car and then made her way into the clinic, screwing up her courage to face Matt, but Elle waylaid her. 'Matt's at the hospital, operating.'

'He does that?' Joanna was blown away.

'Sometimes.' Elle twitched a shoulder. 'They call him in if there's an emergency—the tricky ones there's no time to send on.'

'Oh,' Joanna croaked, feeling as though she'd walked on stage without her script.

Elle's tiger gaze widened fractionally. 'Matt's a specialist orthopaedic surgeon. Didn't he tell you?'

'He must have done,' Joanna flannelled like mad.

'You couldn't have been listening.' Elle gave a quick smile. 'By the way, congratulations on your diagnosis of Sasha's problem. We should see a great outcome. *Ciao.*' The physio fluttered a wave and continued on her way down the stairs and into Reception.

Joanna blinked. Elle's veiled hostility appeared to have vanished and it seemed as though she was ready to accept Joanna as one of the team. Matt must have put her in the picture about Sasha. Well, of course he would have, if the child was still coming for physio. Joanna felt her mood lighten fractionally.

Going into her office, she found that Matt had left her a detailed list for the day ahead. How like him.

He was so ordered about everything. So obviously accepting. So good at plain soldiering on.

Well, what else had she expected him to do? Yell at her? Start throwing things? She gave a little shake of her head. Of course not. For now, like Matt, she'd soldier on the best way she could, even if it meant dragging her courage up from the floor and just getting on with it.

When Matt returned from the hospital he was polite and professional, and Joanna ached inside for him— for them. But she could think of nothing to say, think of no way to clear the air, no way to start building bridges.

And on Saturday evening, She and Jason went to the Phillipses'.

'Mum's insulin's due at nine.' Earnestly, Steffi briefed Joanna for the evening.

Joanna bit back a smile. 'I'm sure I'll manage, Stef.'

'I'm sorry I couldn't give you more notice.' Steffi looked young and pretty in black velvet pants, a cobwebby silk shirt and multicoloured waistcoat. 'You didn't have anything planned, did you?'

'Not a thing,' Joanna lied. She hugged Steffi around the shoulders. 'I'm so glad you're having an evening out, Stef. Anyone I know?'

'An old school friend, actually.' Steffi shoved a few bits and pieces into a soft little purse. 'Kerry Anderson. She's been working in England for the last year, but we've kept in touch. There's a group of us meeting for a meal. A few drinks, a few laughs. Should be fun.'

Joanna's brown eyes softened. That was just what

Steffi needed. Suddenly, it seemed right that she and Jason had become involved with this family.

'His nibs and Mum seem to be getting on like a house on fire.' Steffi flicked her head towards the lounge room from where Jason's rapidly fired questions and Corin Phillips's measured replies could be clearly heard. She winked, swiping up her keys from the hall table. 'Your son's a real heartbreaker, isn't he?'

'You'd better believe it.' Joanna didn't know whether to laugh or cry at the irony.

Sasha arrived for her appointment. Joanna had been seeing her young patient on a weekly basis for several weeks now. Each time they'd used Elle's office because Joanna had the feeling Sasha was most comfortable there.

Now, however, Joanna had put her own bits and pieces about her own domain and had made it what she'd termed people-friendly, and today she'd decided she would talk to Sasha there. She was delighted to see her almost jumping out of her skin.

'Hey, this is cool!' Sasha's bright gaze went right round the room.

In her new work environment, Joanna had striven for simplicity. She'd had a rummage round at home and gathered up a few items, like the geranium in an earthenware pot which she'd stencilled with artistic splodges and pretty leaves.

Her next find had been the upright wicker basket which she'd turned into a table. First she'd got Jason to help her fill it with sand to weigh it down and keep it steady. Then she'd paid a visit to her local DIY store where she'd had a piece of glass cut specially for the top. It was here she'd placed her huge floral arrangement.

She'd thought long and hard about that. Knowing she couldn't afford weekly bunches of fresh flowers, she'd decided to mix fresh blooms with artificial and had been more than pleased with the effect she'd created.

Sasha, too, seemed to approve of the décor wholeheartedly. 'So, who's this?' She skipped across to Joanna's desk and picked up a framed photograph.

'My son, Jason,' Joanna's gaze was gentle on the now bright-eyed Sasha. 'He attends Blaxland College.'

'Cool.' Sasha replaced the photograph carefully. 'I go to Girls' Grammar.' She darted away towards the window, angling one knee up on the window-seat to peer out. 'Check this out! You can see the park from here. And there's Mum down there, waiting for me.' She seemed pleased with her discovery.

'Are you going to let me check *you* out today?' Joanna asked teasingly. 'Or is this just a flying visit?' She began to unravel her sphygmomanometer from its case.

'I'm heaps better.' Sasha slid into the chair beside Joanna and rolled her sleeve up obligingly.

Joanna quickly pumped to get a pressure reading. 'I can see you are.' A hundred on seventy. Sasha was really on her way. Her pulse of seventy-eight confirmed that her young body was turning itself around quickly. Thank God. Joanna made the notation in her file and then looked up with a query. 'Things are going well, then?'

'Pretty well.' Sasha considered. 'I'm not allowed back at gym yet but I'm not bothered. Dad says I should switch to ice-skating instead.'

So her father had become involved. Joanna was relieved and delighted for the young girl. 'Does that appeal to you?'

'Kind of. You have to be really strong in your legs for that. And I am. Or I will be again soon,' she added with youthful confidence.

'And with your gymnastics training for balance and so on, it would be a natural progression to skating, wouldn't it?' Joanna was glad she'd boned up on her subject before Sasha's visit.

'Oh, I can skate already,' the youngster dismissed airily. 'It's a cool sport and the costumes are excellent. Nicer than gym wear.'

Such was the inconstancy of youth. Joanna schooled her expression before she said cautiously, 'There's something else, Sasha. I've had a chat with your mum about it but the decision is ultimately yours. I'd like to start you on a low-dosage contraceptive pill to regulate your periods.'

Sasha's eyebrows touched her white-blonde fringe. 'I haven't got them back yet.'

'And you probably won't until you put on at least three or four more kilos.'

Sasha seemed to be thinking. 'So, would I have to take the pill for ever?'

'No, of course not. Only until your system's back on track. Your hormones are all over the place at the moment. But even when everything is regulated again, don't take it on yourself to just stop taking the Pill,' Joanna warned. 'Come and talk to me first and we'll work out a plan for you to ease back gradually. That's very important, Sasha. So, no cold turkey, OK?'

'OK.' Sasha's gaze flicked towards Jason's photograph. 'Is your son going to be a doctor like you?'

'Don't think so.' Joanna's little chuckle was dry. 'I think he sees himself as some kind of high-profile sportsperson earning lots of money.'

'That would be so cool!'

Joanna twitched a hand. 'Don't roll your sleeve down yet. We have to take another blood sample today.'

'Why are we doing this again?' Sasha gritted her teeth, watching ghoulishly as Joanna pricked a vein and drew out the blood.

'To check where your haemoglobin levels are presently. And we'll go on testing you over the next three to six months until you're right back to where you should be. Are you managing to tolerate the iron preparation?'

Sasha made a small face. 'It's a bit yucky but I drown it with banana smoothie.'

Joanna chuckled, placing the labelled blood to one side for collection. 'You're going OK with your eating plan, then?'

'Mrs Groves gave Mum heaps of recipes,' Sasha confirmed, whirling off her chair and to her feet. She looked down at the floor for a moment. 'I...guess it will be OK about the Pill. Will you give me a script?'

'Yes, Sasha, I can do that. And before you begin taking it, we'll get your mum to sit in and go over everything again.'

With Sasha's departure, Joanna wandered across to

the window, her thoughts locked in and a bit melancholy. As she stood gazing out, Sasha appeared from the shadow of the building and crossed the road to the park.

Joanna blinked, watching as Gerri Wardell unravelled her long legs and stood up from the park bench. She held out her arms to her daughter, hugged her when she got there and dropped a kiss on the top of her head.

Joanna bit her lips together. It felt almost like intruding on their privacy but she didn't draw back. Couldn't for some reason. Instead, her eyes stayed glued on the tableau of mother and child.

Sasha's bright little face turned upwards to her mother's. She said something. Something that made her mother nod and toss her head back in a laugh. They hugged again and then, arms linked, they set off through the park.

The moment was over. Joanna's heart was touched beyond belief. One little family that looked like surviving. She gave a jerky sigh and turned away from the window, thinking, This is what it's all about. This unbreakable bond between mother and child. It's not odd or threatening.

But why couldn't Matt see that's how it was with her and her son? Why couldn't he? She made a sound of pain and frustration in her throat. Perhaps he didn't want to.

Perhaps he'd just plain given up on them.

When her phone rang, she picked it up dispiritedly. 'Joanna Winters.'

'Joanna, it's Debra Carlisle.'

The last person she'd expected to hear from.

Joanna felt a nudge of unease. 'Deb—this is a surprise.'

'I'm in town,' Deb continued without further preamble. 'Could we meet for lunch?'

'Ah…' Joanna flicked up her watch. 'Brunch, you mean.' She laughed. It was eleven-thirty.

'I had an early start this morning,' Deb explained wryly. 'Can you make it?'

'Ah…yes.' And it might be very nice to talk to Matt's sister again. 'Where?'

'The Brown Jug. It's not far from you there, just on the other side of the park.'

'Lovely.' Joanna was immediately looking forward to a brisk walk through the park in the crisp winter sunshine. 'See you there soon.'

'I'm nearby,' Deb said, 'so I'll go in and get a table near the back so we can have a good old natter in peace. Oh, and, Joanna?'

'Yes?'

'Don't say anything to Matt about meeting me, OK?'

CHAPTER EIGHT

JOANNA felt as though she were back at boarding school, sneaking out for a midnight feast.

In order to keep her date with Deb, she'd done a quick make-up repair, swiped a brush through her hair and added a spray of her favourite cologne.

Why was she feeling almost guilty? she wondered, pushing her way out of the building and crossing the road to the park. She was more or less setting her own work agenda these days. She could take her lunch-break whenever she liked.

No, it had been Deb's last little rider not to tell Matt that had her intrigued. Perhaps she wanted to talk about a surprise for him or something? From what Joanna had observed, they seemed pretty close.

Well, no doubt she'd find out soon.

The Brown Jug was one of Glenville's original cafés. With its dark wooden tables and high-back booths, it offered a degree of privacy to its diners.

Deb's face lit in welcome. 'You look fabulous, Joanna.'

'You don't look half-bad yourself,' Joanna reciprocated with a smile. Deb did indeed look attractive in a well-cut navy trouser suit and soft white shirt.

Deb chuckled, waving Joanna into the bench seat opposite her. 'After all this time, holding the fort on my own at Featherdale, I could probably be forgiven for looking like a dishrag.'

'Not a chance. How is Scott, by the way?'

'Home next week.' Deb's happiness was quietly evident. 'He won't be able to do much, of course.'

'At least he'll be able to supervise.'

Deb snorted. 'Give the orders more like. Now, what are we having?' She picked up the buff-coloured menu.

'A toasted sandwich and a pot of tea will suit me fine.' Joanna folded the menu and placed it aside as if it was of little consequence what they ate. She was more interested in why Matt's sister had wanted to see her, and secretly.

'Me, too.' Deb signalled a hovering waitress and gave their order. 'At least we'll be served quickly here and we won't be interrupted.' Resting her chin on her steepled hands, she looked across at Joanna. 'What's eating Matt?'

Joanna smothered a groan. Deb really shot from the hip. 'What makes you think I'd know?'

'Come off it, Joanna.' Deb was blunt. 'You and he were as thick as thieves that night at Featherdale. And afterwards, if I'm any judge,' she added archly.

Joanna coloured faintly. 'We were for a little while,' she said slowly. 'But then things got complicated.'

There was a long pause, which Deb broke with gentle warmth. 'I'm not trying to be nosy, Joanna. But I worry about Matt. I love my twin dearly—'

'You're twins?'

Deb laughed. 'I thought you knew.'

Joanna shook her head. 'But I heard you address Matt as your big brother. I, um, assumed he was older.'

'He is.' Deb gave a snip of laughter. 'By thirty minutes. We've always been close. Told each other stuff. But lately…' She shrugged away the rest of the sentence.

Glad of the diversion, Joanna looked up gratefully when their food came. Although suddenly she'd lost her appetite. But she'd have to make an effort for the look of the thing.

'So, how have things become complicated?' Deb's pretty bracelets jangled as she lifted the silver teapot and poured their tea.

Joanna took a deep breath. 'There's some enmity between Matt and my son, Jason. From regarding Matt as something of a hero, Jase sees him now as— as a rival.'

'For your affections,' Deb added, and clicked her tongue in exasperation. 'But Matt should be able to handle that. He's good with young people. I must say, all this sounds a bit odd, Joanna. Have a sandwich,' she sidetracked. 'They look delicious.'

'Matt doesn't seem to even want to try.' Joanna's mouth twisted slightly. 'It's like he's just switched off, washed his hands of us…'

Deb shook her head mutely. 'Yet for a while there you both seemed so happy. So good together. And I was so thrilled that Matt had found someone again.'

'Again?' Joanna blinked uncertainly.

'Oh, lord, I'm sorry!' Deb's hand shot forward and took Joanna's wrist. 'I'm about as subtle as a sledge-hammer.' She made a dismissive noise. 'He hasn't told you anything, has he?'

Joanna shook her head. 'No.'

'Matt was married once, Joanna. It ended tragically. But that's all I'll say. The rest, if he wants to tell you, will have to come from him.'

'Then I'll just have to find a way to ask him,' Joanna resolved quietly.

And a time and a place, Joanna added silently a bit later. She'd left Deb shortly after her revelation. And stuck her with the bill, she remembered ruefully. But Deb wouldn't mind.

'Good luck, Joanna,' she'd said, her voice reflecting her genuine kindness and concern when Joanna had got abruptly to her feet and gathered up her bag.

Why on earth was she hurrying back? Consciously, she slowed her steps. Since she'd cut short her lunch, she had oceans of time to kill.

And time to decide what was the best course of action to take with Matt.

Her dark head came up, her eyes thoughtfully assessing the flowering gums that lined the meandering path. The park was lovely. Open, flat spaces harmonised gently with hillocks and unexpected little corners of shadowy trees. And benches were situated both in sunshine and shade so that folk had a choice of where to sit.

The sun on her back was warm. Stopping for a moment, Joanna closed her eyes, breathing in the earthy, woody moistness of the little cultivated rainforest of tree ferns and mosses.

Her reverie was rudely interrupted by the trill of her mobile phone. Now what? She sighed inwardly, rescuing it from her blazer pocket and putting it to her ear. She was surprised to hear an excited Jason on the other end.

'Coach wants to take us to the coast tomorrow, Mum. It's a kind of bonding camp for the athletics team. We'll be staying overnight. Is it OK?'

Joanna pulled her thoughts together. 'Yes, I suppose so. Where will you be staying?'

'At the Tallebudgera fitness camp. The vacancy just came up this morning—that's why we've only got short notice. We're travelling in the school bus and two of the teachers are going as support staff.'

'What do you need to take?'

'Not much. Just my sleeping bag, jeans and stuff. And my kit.'

Which was in a rancid heap in the laundry. 'Ah...'

'I'll chuck what I need in the washing machine when I get home,' Jason said helpfully, as though homing in on her hesitation. 'I can go, can't I?'

'Well, seeing you're Blaxland's up-and-coming sports champ, I guess you'd better.' Joanna was suddenly light-hearted, walking on air. She now had a time, a place and an opportunity to talk to Matt.

Thank you, God.

Knowledge gave her strength when she knocked on his office door later that afternoon.

He looked up from his paperwork. 'You just off?'

Oh, lord. He seemed as remote as ever. 'Mmm.' Joanna drummed up a quick smile. 'I'm all squared away.' Her throat dried for a second, before she made her prepared little speech. 'Jason's off on an overnight camp tomorrow. I'd like you to come to dinner.'

He sat for a second, staring at her, and then said tersely, 'Are you giving a dinner party?'

'For two.' She grasped her courage in both hands. 'We have to talk, Matt.'

He began to shake his head but she glared at him and he stopped. 'What time?'

She twitched a shoulder. 'Sixish?'

'Can I bring anything?'

'No, thanks. It won't be fancy,' she warned him. 'I'll throw a casserole together.' She moved away and then turned at the door. 'And don't bother with wine. My parents have a vineyard in the Canberra district. They keep me well supplied.'

What the hell was he doing here? The knot tightened in Matt's stomach as he rang Joanna's doorbell and waited.

Joanna took a deep breath on her way to open the door. She fully expected things to be awkward between them but she had no set plan. She could only hope that some time during the evening the warm and real Matt McKellar would emerge from the coat of armour he'd been wearing lately.

She opened the door with a flourish. Start as you mean to go on, she decided. 'Hi, come on in.'

Matt's gaze narrowed marginally on her before he stepped over the threshold.

'Can I take your jacket?' There was a sleety rain falling.

'Thanks,' he said, his voice sounding rusty and unused. 'Something's smells good,' he added a bit halfheartedly, and followed her through to the kitchen.

'I reneged on the casserole and made soup. It's a nice thick one and I've some zucchini bread to go with it.' She stopped, aware her heart was hammering and she felt faintly sick. But she couldn't seem to stop her tongue chattering on.

'Could you open the wine? I...have real trouble with the corks.'

Matt watched helplessly as she turned to open the fridge. The skinny-rib black jumper she wore pulled away from her waistband of her jeans, revealing a strip of pale skin. He took a breath so deep it hurt. 'Joanna...'

She turned in a little jerky movement. He was holding out his arms to her.

Almost in slow motion, she closed the door of the fridge and stood against it. Then she ran to him.

'These have been the longest weeks of my life,' he sighed, wrapping her to him, his words muffled against her hair.

'Oh—for me, too,' she whispered against his chest.

'I've wanted you, Joanna...so much, so badly...' He spoke as if the air were being pushed out of his body.

'Matt...' She leant away from him, staring up into his eyes, an odd little spiral of trepidation making her words husky. 'You and me. It's not that simple... Is it?'

He tensed. 'Jason?'

'No.' She faced him with uncertainty and wariness clouding her eyes. 'Deb...talked to me yesterday.'

'And?' He turned her shoulders a fraction.

'Before we can move forward, I think you have things to tell me...'

Matt closed down, pulling his arms away as if she'd struck him. He swung to the window, peering sightlessly at the rain, his hands shoved deeply into his pockets.

Joanna grasped her courage in both hands. She

went to him, moved close to him so that their arms were touching. 'Talk to me, Matt. Please…'

His jaw worked and it seemed he would ignore her plea. After an eternity he said, 'There's nothing you can do, Joanna.'

'Probably not. But I can listen. I've been there, too, remember?'

'Not like this you haven't.'

'Oh, spare me!' Joanna felt the sudden core of anger in her chest. 'I lost someone I loved, too! My husband was just a boy! He didn't deserve to die either!'

He was silent for a long moment then he let his breath out in a ragged sigh. 'How much did Deb tell you?'

'Not much.' She swallowed. 'Just that you've been married—and that it ended tragically. I gather your wife died.'

'Yes.' He pulled his hands from his pockets and held them stiffly at his sides. 'All right, I'll tell you about Nicola. But it's not pretty.'

'When a young person dies, for whatever reason, it's never pretty.' She took his hand, tightening her fingers in his. And then, as if guided by remote control, they walked back through to the lounge.

Joanna tugged him gently down onto the big old chesterfield in front of the fire. 'Let it go now,' she coaxed gently. 'All of it.'

Matt took a great shuddering breath and then he did.

'It's nearly seven years ago now. Nicola was twenty-six. I was thirty, studying towards my speciality. We were expecting our first child and about to buy our first home. We'd seen one we were pretty keen on and Nic suggested we have another look.'

He stopped and breathed again. 'She rang me at the hospital to tell me she'd teed it up with the estate agent and she'd pick me up at the end of my shift. I wasn't keen for her to be out driving. We'd had rain and the roads…

'It was winter, about four-thirty in the afternoon. The smash happened outside the hospital. Nic was turning to come into the car park, a van delivering linen sideswiped her and rammed her car into a wall.'

'Oh, no…' Joanna felt shock drain the blood from her face. She wrapped her arms around Matt's waist and held him. After the longest time, she felt him begin to relax slightly. 'Do you want to go on?' she asked quietly.

He took a ragged breath. 'Maybe I should. I need to tell you, I think.'

She gave him a squeeze of encouragement and after a bit he began again.

'It was surreal—like a nightmare. The rain and the rescue guys in their orange slickers—doctors…' He paused, his intake of breath visibly painful. 'She was in Theatre for six hours but in the end they couldn't save her. They managed to get the baby out. A little boy. He…was too immature to survive. He lasted only a few hours. But he was beautiful, quite perfect. I had him baptised. I, um, named him Nicholas Matthew.' He turned to Joanna, his face streaked with tears. 'I think she would have liked that.'

On a little moan, he turned in her arms, dropping his head against hers and holding her for dear life against his chest.

In the end, Joanna didn't know who was holding who the tightest. But she knew right at that moment she didn't want to be anywhere else.

Finally, Matt seemed to pull himself together. 'Sorry.' He looked away, awkward now. 'That all got a bit messy.'

'You've never grieved properly, have you, Matt?' she asked carefully and with some perception.

'Maybe not…'

'You didn't seek counselling?'

He gave a stiff laugh. 'You know what doctors are like—useless about their own health and welfare.'

'What about having a chat with Sally Ekersley?' Joanna crossed her fingers.

'Yes…OK…' The words punched the air like a heavy sigh. 'That might be a good idea.'

She rubbed her head against his shoulder. 'Like that drink now?'

He squeezed her hand. 'Thanks. But I didn't get to open the wine for you.' Straightening up, he levered himself out of the sofa. 'I'll do it now.'

'Would you prefer a Scotch?'

He gave a rueful smile. 'How did you guess?'

They moved quietly and gently through the rest of the evening. Joanna lit some candles and put on some Spanish guitar music that melted into the background.

With a little flourish she dished up the soup, adding a sprinkle of fresh herbs across the top. Matt broke the bread and they ate off trays in front of the fire.

The rain continued to fall and the night drew in around them. 'Why don't I make some coffee?' Joanna swung her feet to the floor. Somehow she'd become wedged against Matt and one of her legs had pins and needles. 'Ouch!'

'Here, let me rub it.' Matt hoisted her feet onto his lap and began working his fingers up and down her calf muscle. 'Better?' He gave her a fleeting smile.

'Much.'

'Stay here, then. I'll make the coffee.'

'No, I should walk around,' she insisted. 'Help me up, Matt.'

He did, turning her to face him, spreading his hands over her hips and looking deeply into her eyes. 'Thank you, Joanna,' he said, his voice gruff and not quite even.

She nodded, knowing what he meant. No further words were necessary.

They made the coffee together and Joanna opened a packet of chocolate biscuits. She wrinkled her nose at him. 'Can't have you going without your energy hit.'

His lopsided smile was edged with vulnerability. 'You're getting to know me so well.'

'Would that be such a bad thing?'

He didn't answer.

They were halfway through their coffee when Matt said quietly, 'Tell me about Jason's father.'

'Damon.' Joanna's voice softened over the name. 'He was lovely. We met when I'd just completed my HSC—Higher School Certificate for you Queenslanders.'

Matt chuckled. 'We call it Senior Certificate. Go on with your story.'

'I'd just turned eighteen. Damon was twenty. We met at a party. Damon was there celebrating being picked for the state rugby squad. We connected—it was as simple as that. Six months later we were married.'

'Your parents didn't object?'

'Strenuously. But not because they didn't like Damon—everyone did. They thought we were both too young. But we knew we wanted to be together, properly married—not just living together.' Her mouth lifted in a token smile. 'That probably sounds a bit old-fashioned.'

'On the contrary. It sounds very Joanna-ish.' Matt took her hand, kissing it on the way to his lap. 'And that's meant as a compliment.'

'Thanks.' She took a sip of her coffee and leaned over to place the mug on the side table. 'We had a nice little town house in Canberra. I'd begun at university. Damon was involved with his sporting commitments and studying part time. Life was busy and we were as happy as larks.' Her voice faded and then she went on quietly, 'Six months later, Damon was diagnosed.'

'Oh, God...' Matt closed his eyes, picturing her heartache.

'Yes, well, the cancer was very aggressive. He, um, died within three months.'

'Was there nothing they could do?'

Joanna shook her head. 'Nothing that could halt it. And don't forget we're talking about the situation years ago. We've come a long way with cancer research since then.'

His knuckles brushed her cheek. 'How did you bear it?'

Joanna lifted her head and smiled through the sheen

of tears that had sprung out of nowhere. She brushed them away with the tips of her fingers. 'We spent every minute we could together. Damon was so strong spiritually—and I leant on him when it probably should have been the other way round. I was pregnant by then. And we discussed names—Katie for a girl, Jason if I was carrying a boy...'

'He'd have been very proud of Jason,' Matt said generously.

'Yes, he would. The end was swift but we'd said our goodbyes long before. And it was all right. He had no more pain.'

For a long time then they clung together, letting their memories push past the blockade they'd struggled to make emotion-tight.

Eventually, Matt murmured against her temple, 'We've been a couple of weeping willows tonight, haven't we?'

'But it's been good, though, hasn't it? Cleansing.'

'Mmm.' Matt tangled his fingers in hers and linked them over his heart. 'Like a dose of salts.'

'Peasant!' Lifting their entwined hands, Joanna thumped his chest.

'Ouch!' He pretended to fall backwards, taking her with him so that she landed on top of him. She put her face down to his and they pressed foreheads, touched noses. And laughed softly. It was laughter born of pain, the pain of remembering. But having remembered and let go, they could now begin to heal.

It was late and the fire had all but gone out.

Matt roused himself, unwinding himself off the sofa, pulling her upright with him. He looked down at her, lifting his hands to bracket her face. 'I should make tracks...'

A breathless pause while she took the words in. Then she said softly, 'I don't think so, Doctor.' She raised her hands, burying them in the soft thick hair at his nape. 'If you think I'm turfing you out in that rain, think again.'

A beat of silence.

'Joanna?' He said her name with a rich huskiness that rippled along her skin.

'Yes,' she breathed, leaving him in no doubt what she wanted, hearing her own heartbeat, already feeling the imprint of his body on hers. And recognising the ripples of her own need, she clung to him.

Matt steadied her head, kissing her with a slow series of caresses, a delicate, tormenting exploration, the touch of his mouth feather-like, silken, intoxicating.

Joanna wound her arms more tightly around him, revelling in the muscled contours of his back, the ridges that flexed beneath her fingertips. A king tide of need overcame her, shocking her in its intensity.

Drawing back, she whispered his name as the firelight made soft shadows on the wall and ceiling.

She woke as early morning filtered through the chinks in the blinds, flashbacks of the night coming back in a rush of remembered pleasure of the kind of passion she'd all but forgotten.

Matt.

She leaned up on her elbow to gaze at him. His dark hair was askew, sticking up in little tufts. She smiled. He looked absurdly youthful, so vulnerable in sleep. As she continued to watch him, his eyes opened, their direct blueness flooding her body with warmth.

'Good morning.' He shifted closer, nuzzling the side of her throat, while his hand slid up her rib cage to encircle her breast.

'Morning…' The greeting was indistinct, happening a breath before their lips met and clung, beginning a whole new voyage of tender exploration that set her senses spinning away and afterwards pondering soberly her great good fortune at having twice in a lifetime found her soul mate.

A long time later, they lay face to face, their arms loosely linked around each other.

'What are we going to do this morning?' Matt asked lazily, his fingers in her hair, gathering it up and letting it tumble away. 'Shall we have breakfast in bed?'

'Please—no!' Joanna pretended to shudder. 'After enduring Mother's Day breakfasts in bed over ten or more years, I've kind of gone off it.'

Matt chuckled. 'Tell me about it.'

'Oh, Jason used to bring me a cup of tea made with hot water from the tap. And burnt toast with big holes in the middle where he'd tried to spread the butter straight from the fridge.'

'Ye gods. Did you eat it?'

'Of course I ate it.' Her eyes became soft. 'He was such a sweet little boy.'

'And now he's almost a foot taller than you.'

'Kids grow up so fast, don't they?'

'Yes, they do.'

His voice had become wistful and Joanna wondered if he was thinking of his little boy who had never made it to manhood. 'I made a very thoughtless comment to you once, Matt.'

'Did you?' he murmured, and she turned her head into the hollow of his shoulder and placed a tender kiss on his skin.

'I accused you of never having been a parent. And you went all quiet. I know why now.'

'Water under the bridge. You weren't to know.'

'About then you seemed to give up on us.'

'You and your son seemed a fairly impenetrable unit,' he said gruffly. 'I didn't want to place more pressure on you. It was obvious Jason was taking all your time and energy.'

'But I could have made room for you.'

He eased away from her, stroking her hair back from her face. 'Emotionally, it all got too hard. You were the first woman I'd related to since Nicola. I didn't know where to step, what to think. It just seemed safer to distance myself.'

She made a small contrite sound. 'Thank heavens Deb said something.'

'Oh, sweetheart,' he whispered and, folding her back into his arms, cradled her lovingly against his chest. After a while, he repeated, 'So what are we going to do this morning, Dr Winters?'

Joanna stirred and stretched. 'Read the Sunday papers and have a nice leisurely breakfast?'

He kissed the tip of her nose. 'Sounds good. I'll go out and get the papers while you fix breakfast, then.'

'Hey, wait a minute!' She sent him an indulgent, half-amused look. 'What about a bit of role reversal here? I'll go out and get the papers and you can fix breakfast.'

'Ah…' He smiled lopsidedly. 'Got any cornflakes?'

'When do you expect Jason home?' Matt looked at Joanna over the Sunday supplement. The rain had cleared away, leaving a bright, sparkling morning, and they'd had breakfast on the deck and were lingering over their coffee.

'They were breaking camp at lunchtime, I think,' she responded absently. 'They'll probably be back in Glenville about four. Why?'

Matt's gaze deepened. 'I just wondered how you wanted to play this—us?'

'I hadn't thought…' It had all seemed so natural to have Matt here this morning. So right. In fact, she'd gone so far as to wondering when he'd want to move in.

'Perhaps we shouldn't be too overt around Jason at this point,' he said carefully.

'You mean you don't want to come to the house?' Joanna's rapidly fired question mirrored her surprise.

Matt didn't answer directly. 'Jason has a fair bit on his plate at the moment. Before he went off me, we had a few good talks. He's set his long-term goal on earning a living through sport. And with his inherited physical attributes and his own natural talent, he's got a more than fair chance of succeeding.'

She lowered her gaze. 'He's very keen to get a scholarship to the Australian Institute of Sport in Canberra.'

'There you are, then.'

A frown flickered in her eyes. 'None of that can

happen until he's finished high school at the end of next year, Matt.'

'But from here on, in order to have some credentials when he applies, he has to make every post a winner, beginning with this inter-schools athletics meet coming up.'

'How did you know about that?'

His mouth compressed for a moment. 'I've been approached to provide the medical cover for the event. Will you be going?'

'Purely as a parent,' Joanna specified. 'Unless you want me as back-up?'

'No, of course not.' His reply was gruff. 'You're entitled to have time off to watch your son compete.'

Joanna smiled, although it cost her an effort. Why did she feel there was some kind of subplot here? Something he was keeping to himself? 'So, what point are you making, then?'

'Right now, Jason needs to keep focused.' Matt's gaze stayed firmly averted. 'He doesn't need distractions.'

'So you'd rather he didn't know about us,' Joanna said flatly.

'Joanna, we're the adults here.' Reaching across, he laid his hand over hers and squeezed. 'We can wait.'

She swallowed. 'How long did you have in mind?'

'Not long.' His mouth compressed for a moment. 'Just long enough for Jason to get his athletics meet over. He's championship material, sweetheart. He needs his chance.' Matt paused, leaning back in his chair and folding his arms. 'Look, I have no hidden agenda here. I just don't want to be the cause of Jason getting distracted and stuffing up his sporting future. I care about both of you too much to let that happen.'

Joanna was touched. 'Do you, Matt?' she asked softly.

'Of course I do.' He was still for a moment, then he let his breath go in a ragged sigh. 'Joanna, I have to take a back seat for the moment and our plans may have to stay on hold for a while, that's all.'

She nodded slowly, understanding. Their time would come. Somehow, she'd have to hang on to that thought.

CHAPTER NINE

A BIT dispiritedly, Joanna tidied up from her last patient of the day. Two weeks on from the magic of discovering how much they meant to each other, she and Matt had made love only once.

Chance would be a fine thing, she huffed silently, swinging her chair round to the computer to bring her notes up to date on her patient, Karen Trevor. The young athlete was suffering from premenstrual tension, but in such an extreme form it was affecting her capacity to train and perform.

With several big meets scheduled over the next twelve months, Karen had been in a state, wondering how on earth she was going to compete and keep faith with her sponsors.

Drastic problems needed drastic solutions, Joanna decided, her preferred course of action being to try altering the timing of the young woman's menstruation. It required quite involved advanced planning and the taking of a suitable progesterone-only contraceptive at a set time during the cycle prior to the one to be altered.

She tapped in the last of her notes. But before she did anything, she'd consult with Matt. And before they did anything at all, Karen would need clearance from a gynaecologist.

She thought of Matt as she drove home. It was only a week since they'd taken a longer than usual lunch-break and gone to his flat. But somehow it seemed like a year.

'I want you so badly, I'm afraid I'll hurt you,' he'd breathed, his control drawn so taut he was shaking.

'You won't hurt me...' She'd reached up and stroked the lean length of his back. 'I need you just as much...'

Oh, lord, she fretted, where will it all end?

'I'm home,' she called, and Jason appeared like magic from his bedroom. 'What's happened?' One keen look had told her that her son was bubbling with subdued excitement.

Jason, grinning broadly, dangled a piece of paper in front of her. 'I won the history essay competition!'

Joanna dropped her bag and hugged him. 'Well done, you! That's brilliant! When are we off to Sydney?'

He looked awkward for a second. 'It's the weekend after next, but I've, um, called Grandad Winters to go with me. You're not into science that much and I thought—'

'Hey, that's OK.' Joanna felt immediately guilty at her relief. With her son away she could have time with Matt. 'So, where is Grandad meeting you?'

'He'll fly in from Canberra and we'll meet at the airport. It'll be excellent!'

And for her and Matt, too. Joanna couldn't wait to tell him next morning. 'Fancy a weekend just to ourselves?' She explained the circumstances.

His smile was worth waiting for. 'A whole weekend!'

Joanna reached out and caressed his face. 'It's hardly a whole weekend, I suppose. Jason flies to

Sydney on Saturday morning and he's back again on Sunday afternoon.'

His lips brushed hers lightly, like thistledown. 'It's a lot more than we've had lately, though, isn't it? Let's go out somewhere fancy on the Saturday night. I want to show you off.'

Life had the darnedest way of altering your plans, Joanna was to think wryly the following week. A phone call from Steffi Phillips began it all.

'Joanna, could I come and see you?' Steffi was hesitant.

'Professionally?' Joanna was immediately concerned.

'Ah, no, not really. I need to talk and you said if I did…'

'I'm free after four this afternoon, Stef. Can you make it then?'

Steffi could.

'So, what's going on?' Joanna had sat Steffi down near the window in her office and poured them each a coffee.

Steffi made a small face. 'I hate working at the Strachan these days—well, it's not the Strachan any more,' she retracted. 'It's now called Northside 24. Because it's open twenty-four hours a day,' she explained.

Joanna looked taken aback. 'It sounds more like the name of a motel.'

'It may as well be,' Steffi huffed disparagingly. 'With patients and staff coming and going all over the place. It's not the same at all. I hate it. And my hours are all over the place as well…'

Joanna could sense the young woman's desperation. Life for Steffi had improved so much over the last few months. It would be a shame to see her feeling overwhelmed again. She took a thoughtful mouthful of her coffee, wondering how she could help.

Suddenly, and with blinding clarity, the solution came to her. 'Would you like to come and work here, Stef? We're desperate for a friendly, efficient office manager.'

'Here?' Steffi squeaked, and took a moment to take it in. Then her face fell. 'You're just being kind as usual, Joanna. Manufacturing a job for me.'

'Listen to me.' Leaning forward, Joanna took Steffi's wrist. 'We've been managing piecemeal for office help for ever. We all do what we can ourselves and Matt sends the less confidential bits out to an agency, but it would be the answer to a prayer if you could see your way clear to come and work here. It really would.'

Eyes alight, Steffi clasped her hands to her chest. 'Are you sure? Won't you have to run it past Dr McKellar or something?'

Joanna's head went back in a laugh. 'I'll tell him I've found us an office angel. He'll go along with that.'

'I'd love the job, then.' Steffi whirled up from her chair. 'I don't even want to know the terms and conditions. I know they'll be fair.' She grinned. 'It'll be fab, working with you again, Joanna. And I'll start as soon as I can,' she promised. 'Oh—there was one other thing.' Steffi went a bit pink. 'Could you and Jason sit with Mum on Saturday night? Kim Newlands has asked me out. Well, our birthdays are only a couple of days apart...'

'And you'd like to celebrate together,' Joanna added kindly, seeing her own 'fancy' evening out with Matt vanish like leaves in the wind. 'Tell your mum it'll be just me, though. Jason's off on his prize trip to Sydney.'

'Oh, yes, the essay competition. He told us. Isn't it exciting for him?'

'It certainly is.' Again, Joanna wondered about life's ironies as she walked Steffi out through Reception.

'I'll come with you,' Matt said, when Joanna told him the enforced change to their plans, 'if it's all right with everyone.'

Joanna's face lit up. 'Oh, I'm sure it will be. And if we go a bit earlier, it'll be a good chance for you to meet Steffi and reassure her about the job here.' She bit her lip. 'I'm sorry about the restaurant but I have a kind of open-ended arrangement with Stef—'

'Hush…' Matt placed a gentle finger across her lips. 'We'll be together, Joanna, no matter where we spend the evening. And that's all I care about,' he murmured, gathering up a handful of her hair to expose the side of her throat for his kiss.

The day of the inter-schools sports came round far more quickly than Joanna was prepared for. She stifled a sigh. These days her life seemed unusually compartmentalised and she worried she was spreading herself too thinly between her son, her lover and her work.

Jason refused all but a high-energy protein-supplement drink for breakfast. Joanna recognised the signs. Her son was strung competition-tight, pumping out adrenalin like mad.

'You know Matt is the MO for the meet today?' She tried to sound casual, eyeing Jason evenly over the rim of her coffee mug.

'Yeah, they told us at school.' Jason downed the last of his drink, wiping his mouth with the back of his hand. 'He's the logical choice. I don't have a problem with it.'

No, only with the possibility of your mother becoming close to him. Joanna lowered her gaze. 'What time is your event?'

'They'll run the heats first thing. Finals about eleven.'

'So you'll get the sprint over before lunch,' Joanna clarified.

He nodded. 'I'll stoke up a bit before the long jump in the afternoon. What time are you getting there?'

Matt had talked of them going together but she'd vetoed that. This day belonged to her son. She smiled. 'In time for your heat.'

He nodded, pulling in a hard breath. 'I'll, uh, see you there, OK?' He began to move towards the door.

'Jase…' Joanna quickly put her coffee down and went to him. Placing her hands on his shoulders, she looked earnestly into his young eyes. 'You can only give it your best shot, love. You've done all the preparation. You've trained hard and you're fit.'

'Yeah, I know all that.' Jason gave her an awkward grin. 'But I'll win, Jo. Just watch me.'

*   *   *

The playing fields at Blaxland looked a picture. Despite a rather frosty start to the morning, the sun was now out and already gathering strength.

Joanna nosed her car into the designated parking area, wondering whether Matt had arrived yet. Swinging out of the car, she locked it and looked around her, her eyes feasting on the expansive flower-beds bursting with a riot of winter roses, stocks and creamy chrysanthemums.

'Hi…' Matt had come up unobtrusively behind her.

Joanna spun round and her face lit with pleasure. She would have hugged him if she'd dared. 'I wondered if you'd got here,' she said instead.

'Mmm.' He looked away. 'I've had the tour. The facilities seem excellent.'

'That's reassuring.' Joanna gave a rueful laugh. 'I'm glad those horrendous fees I pay are going towards something useful.'

Matt stabbed his fingers through his hair. 'How's Jason?'

'Strung tight, focused, determined he's going to win.'

'Our strategy's paying off, then.' The words were softly spoken, a bit throaty. For a long moment they looked at each other. Suddenly, Matt shook his head as if to clear it. 'I'll park myself somewhere near the first-aid tent. I'll be there if you need me for anything.'

'Shouldn't think so.' Her heart in her eyes, Joanna watched him go. Who was she kidding? She needed him like parched earth needed rain. She turned away, her mind suddenly a jumble of thoughts, longings and emotions.

Exchanging greetings here and there, she took her place amongst the other parents and supporters who were rapidly filling every space along the sides of the running track.

After what seemed like hours, Joanna had cheered herself hoarse and Jason had won his final. Unable to contain herself, and ignoring the rules, she ran towards the finishing line. 'Jase!' she shrieked, finding him at last among the crowd. 'Congratulations!'

'Thanks, Mum.' He was pulling in hard breaths, propped forward, warming down.

'That was magic!' Joanna felt pride almost choke her. '*You* were magic!'

'Yeah, right.' His shrug was embarrassed but she could tell he was chuffed. 'Told you I'd do it, didn't I?'

'You certainly did it.' She put a hand on his back, finding it tacky with perspiration. Her motherly feathers fluffed. 'Shouldn't you get back into your tracksuit now?'

'Don't sweat it, Mum, OK?' He turned away, grinning when several of his team-mates thumped him across the shoulders in congratulations. All high on adrenalin, they began playfully pushing and shoving one another and then bounded away into the crowd.

Joanna felt suddenly bereft, left behind. Out of nowhere her eyes misted. 'Oh, lord,' she murmured, and took a huge shaky breath. Her son was growing up so fast, off about his own business. She would do well to remember that.

She looked around for Matt. She needed a hug. But in the scheme of things that wasn't possible either. A bit disconsolately, she began making her way slowly towards one of the refreshment tents. She needed a cup of tea to restore her equilibrium.

Ten minutes later, Joanna was enjoying her tea and home-made apple strudel. She'd taken herself off to sit under one of the colourful umbrellas dotted about the lawn. Her thoughts were of her son and faintly wistful. The years had sped by so quickly...

It was almost surreal, then, when she turned her head and saw him running towards her across the lawn. It took her a moment to register. 'Jase?' She'd sensed an urgency she couldn't explain and whirled to her feet, an instant knot of unease in her stomach.

'Oh, Mum...' Jason jerked to a stop in front of her, his hands clenched at his sides.

'What is it?' Joanna felt the pinch of nerves turn to an avalanche. The boy was staring at her, his face white and crumpling uncontrollably. 'Jason!' Joanna shook his arm. He was obviously in shock.

'Two of the guys...'

'Yes!' her voice snapped at him. 'Two of the guys what? Tell me!'

Jason's mouth opened and closed and then he croaked, 'I...think they're dead.'

Joanna froze, but only for a second. 'Where are they?'

'In the lo-locker room.'

'Show me!' Propelling Jason with her, Joanna began running.

One look told her they had trouble of the worst kind. The students were big lads, probably from the senior form. One was in an untidy heap on the tiled floor, the other slumped in a plastic chair outside a shower cubicle.

There were spent needles on the floor beside them.

'Get Matt!' Joanna rapped, her face intense.

Beside her, Jason gave a keening little cry.

'Now, Jason!' Joanna screamed at him, shocking him out of his inertia. 'The first-aid tent! Tell him it's drugs—run!'

Left alone, Joanna's gut clenched and clenched again. But in a flash her training had smothered her fear. She needed triage here, and urgently. Instinct told her the boy on the floor was critical. He was frighteningly still, his skin almost blue. She felt for a pulse. Nothing.

She leapt across to the other boy. His breathing was shallow, his pulse hardly palpable but at least it was there. Her heart jerked. She should get him into a left lateral recovery position but his bulk against her eight stone something made it impossible.

Dear God…

She looked wildly around, grabbing several track jackets off their hooks and draping them over him. Try to keep him warm. She knew she was buying time. Her legs shaking, she dropped to the boy on the floor.

'Matt!' She looked up, the expulsion of his name shrieking relief. 'Over here!'

'What the hell?' In a few strides Matt was through the door and hunkering down beside the youth. 'What've we got, Joanna?'

'No pulse, no breath sounds. We'll need adrenalin.'

'Bloody young idiots…' Matt swore softly. But there was no time to sit in judgment. He dived into his case, locating and ripping open the dose of adrenalin, already prepared in its mini-jet. With swift precision, he sent the injection home to the youth's inner arm.

'Let's hope it works, and soon.' Joanna threw herself astride the youth's prostrate form and began CPR, counting the rhythmic beats in her head, almost despairing that it was all too late. Dear heaven, what a waste of a young life...

'Keep it going, Joanna!' She heard the urgency in Matt's voice, felt his fingers hard on her shoulder. 'I'll start bagging him.'

Joanna longed to ease her neck and shoulders, but there was no time for that luxury. She had to keep the lifesaving compressions going.

Matt had the resus bag attached to the small oxygen cylinder and was manually ventilating their patient.

'Anything?' Joanna's heart felt like a jackhammer against her ribs.

Matt shook his head. 'This is a nightmare... And where the hell is the ambulance?'

Thirty seconds later.

'I have a pulse.' Matt's voice was steady, his brow furrowed in concentration. 'But no breath. Stop compressions, Joanna, and take over the bagging. I'll get a line in and then I'll look at the other kid.'

'Oh, my God!' Cathy Lowe, the school nurse, burst in, an ashen-faced Jason following. Cathy's hand went to her throat. 'What's happened?'

'As you see.' Matt's face was like granite. 'We have one student in respiratory arrest but we've managed to get a pulse back. The other lad's unconscious and in a coma.'

'That's Michael Jeffreys.' Cathy's horrified gaze went to the boy on the floor. 'Is he—?'

'In big trouble,' Matt cut in darkly.

'His father's the local vet—Tom Jeffreys.' Cathy was shaking her head as though she couldn't quite believe her eyes.

Warning bells began ringing in Matt's brain and pieces of the jigsaw began fitting together. 'That's probably where they got the dope, then.'

The nurse gasped in disbelief. 'Steroids?'

'What else?' Matt's mouth had a grim little twist. He whipped a cannula into the second boy. 'What's this hero's name? Anyone know?'

'Dean Rolleston.' Jason's voice was hardly above a whisper. 'He's a boarder.'

'And a bloody fool,' Matt ground out relentlessly. 'Jason, you don't need to be here.' His direction was terse, allowing no room for argument.

'What can I do?' Cathy was brisk and professional, breaking the tension.

'Relieve Joanna,' Matt snapped. 'She's borne the brunt of all this. And what's the word on the ambulance?'

'On its way. There was a pile-up on the highway. The base were going to redirect one a.s.a.p. Joanna?' Cathy moved in to take over the CPR.

'Wait!' Joanna bent to place her cheek near the boy's mouth. 'I've got him! Matt—atropine! Quick!'

Matt's hands moved like lightning, drawing up the drug that would stimulate the boy's heart rate and sending it home in a swift jab.

Joanna rested back on her heels, almost seeing the drug work before their eyes. 'Pulse back to sixty,' she relayed evenly. 'Matt, he's waking up.'

Their young patient was indeed waking up, panic and distress in his eyes.

'It's OK, Michael,' Joanna bent to reassure him. 'You're going to be fine.'

His eyes flicked wide open. 'W-what happened?'

'You tell me, mate.' Anger like a loaded spring coiled in Matt's chest. Snatching an empty syringe up off the floor, he held it in front of the boy's face. 'What did you use—animal steroids?'

Michael whimpered. 'Didn't know…'

'You bet you didn't know!' Matt's eyes burned like blue flames. 'You used enough to kill a draught horse. And your mate's not out of the woods yet—not by a long shot.'

'Matt.' Joanna little cry was anguished. 'Not now.'

The ambulance had been and gone. Michael and Dean were on their way to hospital.

'What's your prognosis on Dean?' Joanna asked, helping Matt repack their medical kit. She felt totally out of kilter, she realised, her nerves stretched to shreds.

Matt grimaced. 'He was as stable as we could get him. He's young and fit. I'd guess he'll pull through.' He began to gather the sharps they'd used for safe disposal later.

'Oh, good, you're both still here.' Cathy Lowe slipped quietly back into the locker room. 'The principal asked if you wouldn't mind having a word in his office.'

Joanna drew in a jagged breath and looked helplessly at Matt. He lifted a shoulder. 'Tell your boss we'll be there in a few minutes, Cathy.'

'Thank you both for coming.' Gordon Ashby moved quickly to usher them inside a little later. 'I've taken the liberty of providing some refreshment. Do help yourselves to coffee as well.' He indicated the cafetière on a trolley.

Joanna saw the generous array of sandwiches and cakes but doubted if she'd be able to swallow anything.

Matt, it seemed, had no such qualms. Taking a sandwich, he bit into it with obvious hunger.

Joanna stole a glance at her watch, startled to see it was two o'clock. No wonder Matt was hungry. He'd probably had nothing since breakfast.

'Dr Winters, Dr McKellar, I'm very grateful for your discretion today.' The principal leaned forward confidentially. 'I know I speak for the whole of the Blaxland community when I say we'd like to keep today's business under wraps if possible.'

'I don't like your chances, Mr Ashby.' Matt was blunt. 'The world and his dog must have seen the ambulance arrive. And I know for a fact there were several sports journalists from the national press gallery here.'

'Quite.' Agitatedly, Gordon Ashby brushed a hand across his greying hair. 'We'll have to be alert, then, and go into damage control when and if it's needed.' He turned to Joanna. 'It was very fortunate Jason found the boys, Dr Winters, otherwise...' He palmed his hands expressively.

'Yes, it was,' Joanna said slowly, the spectre of something sinister sending a river of unease up her backbone. It still wasn't clear to her what her son had been doing there, given that the locker room had been made out of bounds during the meet. Unless Jason had arranged to meet Michael and Dean there... But for what purpose? She swallowed thickly.

Surely *that* was unthinkable!

She swung towards Matt, looking shocked. *Stop it*, the look in his eyes said. Reaching out, he put his hand briefly on hers and squeezed. 'Mind pouring us a coffee?'

'Oh. Of course not.' Joanna stood quickly, as if by the action alone she could dam the terrible unease that was gripping her.

'In view of what's happened today...' Gordon Ashby looked down at his hands clasped in front of him on the desk. 'I'd like to ask you, Dr McKellar, if you'd consider coming here to the school and giving a talk to the boys about the dangers of taking drugs with the idea it will enhance their sporting prowess.'

'I'd be glad to.' Matt nodded his thanks to Joanna as she handed him his coffee. 'But I'm surprised you haven't done it already. This kind of activity amongst sports people is hardly new.'

'It's the first time it's happened here,' the principal said defensively, his sensitivities clearly ruffled.

Matt's look was bone dry. 'That you know of.'

Joanna knew neither of them was hungry but she'd decided to make an effort with dinner anyway, hoping to tempt Jason to eat something. But what she really wanted was for them to get back to some kind of normality, she sighed to herself, whisking eggs for an omelette.

And to do that she had to talk to him.

But she was afraid to. Afraid of the answers he would give her. Still more afraid of those he wouldn't. But, whatever else, she had to give him full marks for courage.

Despite the terrible upset of his day, Jason had won his long-jump event in the afternoon. But he seemed in no mood to celebrate. Joanna cast a quick look at her son. For a moment he seemed like her little boy again, showered, his hair squeaky clean, dressed in his oldest jeans and sweatshirt and curled up with a comic book in the breakfast nook.

'We'll eat in here, shall we, Jase?' Joanna threw a handful of fresh herbs into the omelette.

'Yeah—whatever.' Jason didn't lift his head. And when the doorbell pealed a moment later, he didn't move. Stifling a sigh, Joanna wiped some sticky residue from her fingers and went to answer it.

'Matt…' Her hand went to her throat and her heart rate revved up a notch.

'Thought you might like some company.' He held up a bottle of champagne.

'Oh—OK.' Flushing slightly, she stood back to let him in. 'Matt's here,' she announced with overbright emphasis when they stepped back into the kitchen.

'Hi.' Jason looked up warily.

'Hi, yourself. You did well today.' Matt held out his hand. 'Congratulations.'

'Thanks.' Jason hesitated for a second and then stuck out his hand to grasp Matt's.

'Would you like to eat with us?' Joanna came in quickly, circumventing any tension. 'It's just omelette and I can make a salad of some description.'

'Would you mind?' Matt looked pointedly at Jason.

'OK with me.' A smile, faintly guarded, accompanied his little shrug of compliance.

Joanna felt a surge of relief, likening Matt's adult presence to a very solid rock she could lean on. She caught his eye and he winked. 'Like me to open the champagne?'

'Please. You know how I am with corks.'

'I do.' Matt grinned, nudging her out of the way to get to one of the drawers.

Joanna added another egg to the omelette and found the remnants of some Cheddar cheese. Grated, that would bulk up the meal enough to go round, she thought quickly. Putting the egg mixture aside to sit for a minute, she raided the crisper for a pre-packaged salad mix.

Meanwhile, Matt had got down the flutes from a top cupboard and filled them with the golden wine. 'There you are, champ.' Solemnly, he passed a glass to Jason. 'Joanna?'

'Oh—for me?' Joanna took a tight little breath, wiping her hands quickly on a paper towel before taking the glass from Matt's outstretched hand. 'What are we drinking to?'

'To Jason's success, obviously.' Matt's mouth curved a little and he shot the boy a quick glance.

'To Jason.' Joanna held her glass aloft, her eyes shining with pride.

'Well done,' Matt added with quiet satisfaction.

Embarrassed, Jason bit the edge of his bottom lip through a hesitant smile. 'Thanks. I don't have to make a speech, do I?'

His little effort at humour pulled at Joanna's heart-strings. The past weeks hadn't been easy for him. But, then again, they hadn't been exactly a picnic for her and Matt either. 'No, no speeches.' She put a clamp on her negative thoughts. 'Just let's enjoy our champagne, shall we? And I wouldn't mind a hand with setting the table either.'

They could almost pass for a real family. Joanna dipped into the salad bowl for a curl of lettuce, covertly watching the two males in her life. So far, they'd avoided any stiltedness in the conversation and that, she thought wryly, had probably been due in part to Matt's deft handling of it.

And he'd made himself at home, for which she'd been thankful. Hadn't stood on ceremony. Just parked himself comfortably on one side of the built-in nook, leaving Joanna to perch next to Jason on the other.

'I saw you speaking to Fraser Owens from *Sports Extra* magazine.' Matt directed the statement at Jason and then went back to forking up the last of his omelette. 'Pretty high-profile stuff, wasn't it?'

A flush crept over Jason's cheekbones. 'He's doing a piece on me. Had his photographer with him.' He shrugged offhandedly. 'I did a couple of poses for him.'

'You didn't tell me!' Joanna knuckled an admonishing little tap to his upper arm.

Jason rolled his eyes. 'It was no big deal.'

Matt placed his knife and fork neatly together on his plate. 'On the contrary, Jason, I'd say it was a very big deal. Fraser Owens doesn't talk to just any old sportsperson. Especially, he doesn't interview school kids—no slight intended.' Matt held up his hands to negate any possibility of offence.

'He'd made the connection between my dad's

name and me.' Jason leaned forward, his youthful features suddenly alight. 'Winters,' he added, as if it needed clarification. 'Mr Owens said it'll make a good story. And he saw Dad play rugby a few times when he was a cadet sports journalist.' Jason lifted a shoulder. 'He must have a good memory for names and stuff, 'cos he'd have to be pretty old by now— about forty.'

Matt spluttered into his champagne.

Joanna bit her lips together to stifle her own mirth. After a minute, she said, 'I've some honey and almond ice cream in the freezer. Anyone interested?'

'Yes, please.' Jason's look was a bit sheepish.

'I'll pass, thanks, Joanna.' Matt glanced at his watch. 'In fact, I'd better make tracks. I've a bit of boning up to do before tomorrow.'

Joanna's smile was a little strained. She hadn't wanted him to leave so soon. 'But it's Saturday.'

Matt's look was a clear, calm blue. 'I'm operating.'

Jason's gaze sharpened. 'At the hospital?'

'That's right.' Matt stroked a hand around his jaw. 'Sporting injury to repair.'

'W-will you be seeing how Michael and Dean are while you're there?' Jason dropped his gaze, his index finger making little circles on the white tablecloth.

'As a matter of fact, I called the hospital just before I came over here.' Matt kept his voice level. 'They're stable and they'll recover OK.'

Jason's shoulders slumped heavily, his relief almost palpable. 'Stupid morons.'

'They were,' Matt agreed. 'Incredibly stupid. And they should be eternally grateful to you for finding them when you did. Was it just luck you found them?' Matt's question was couched in the most non-threatening tone, suggesting only the mildest interest. Nevertheless, Joanna's hand flew to her throat, a look of panic in her eyes. She went to open her mouth but Matt sent her a warning look. Leave it, the silent message clearly spelt.

'I'd, um, gone to the locker room to change before my long jump.' Jason's throat tightened before he made faltering eye contact with first his mother and then Matt. 'I'd taken an extra kit to school 'cos I knew I'd be all tacky after my sprint...'

And he had been. Joanna took a shallow breath. She'd felt him and could vouch for that.

'I had my form master's permission to be there but I'd got delayed 'cos the guys were jumping all over me after my win.'

Joanna felt the hairs on the back of her neck stand up. She could vouch for that as well. She'd seen how they'd swarmed round Jason with her own eyes. Oh, thank God, she breathed silently, gripped by a blinding relief.

'I was so scared...' Jason wound his arms around his midriff, the faint tremor in his voice reflecting the depth of his fright. 'When I saw the guys...I nearly threw up. And afterwards...' His throat jerked as he swallowed. 'I kept thinking, What if I'd been too late?'

'But you weren't,' Matt's tone was firmly positive. 'And thanks to your quick action in getting your mother, two young lives were saved.'

'Yeah...' Jason's smile was all crooked and he took another shaky breath. 'You reckon I did OK, then, Matt?'

'Very OK.' Matt's voice roughened.

Blinking rapidly, Joanna looked at her son. 'And I think you did OK, too.' Her voice clogged and she couldn't say any more but the bear hug she gave him, tight and warm, said it all.

A short time later, she walked Matt to the front door. 'You were brilliant in there.' Her voice was low, a bit unsteady. 'There are so many pressures on young people nowadays to perform, I was so afraid Jason might have—'

'Silly girl.' Matt wrapped her into his arms. 'You've raised your son too wisely and too well for him to have been mixed up in anything like drugs.'

She made a small face. 'One part of me—the mother part—was telling me that. But then the doctor part kept reminding me he had access to my bag if he was so minded. He's known for ever where I keep my keys—'

'Enough now.' Lifting his hand, Matt laid a finger gently across her lips. 'No more doubts,' he said firmly. 'I'd rather talk about us.'

'Us?'

'Mmm. You and me, Dr Winters. I think it's time you told Jason we want to get married. Or we could tell him together?'

Joanna stared helplessly up at him. He made it all sound so easy. And surely it should have been. She moistened her lips. 'It's better if I do it, Matt.' She rested her cheek against the comforting wool of his jumper. 'And I will—soon.'

CHAPTER TEN

JOANNA was thoughtful as she logged in the last of her notes. It had been a month since the frightening events at the school.

Fortunately, a scandal had been averted. The media, to their credit, had obviously chosen to ignore it, perhaps deciding that the youths involved deserved a second chance.

The school council had believed that as well. Michael and Dean had been sent for counselling and would not be expelled.

And Matt had given a series of talks to the students. On one such occasion Joanna had slipped in unobtrusively to listen and had been impressed by his warm, down-to-earth approach. He'd undoubtedly communicated with the students on their level. Several had approached him afterwards to ask if they could talk to him privately.

Was it a case of all being well that ended well? she pondered, her head coming up at the tap on her door. It opened and Matt came in.

'I was just thinking about you,' she said softly, gripped by a blinding pleasure at just seeing him standing there. Sliding out of her chair, she ran to him, winding her arms around him.

'Joanna…' Their lips met and clung. 'Is this a good time to talk?' Matt drew slightly away, his hands continuing to knead her spine gently.

'What is it?' She blinked up at him, a slight frown in her eyes. 'You…seem so serious. Are we broke?'

'No.' He huffed a dry laugh. 'But we do need to talk.' He touched a kiss to the curve of her throat. 'Why aren't we married, sweetheart?'

She sighed. 'You know why. Jason—'

'Jason's come round a lot.'

'He's not come back to the club.'

'That's neither here nor there,' Matt dismissed. 'He's concentrating on track and field. He doesn't have time to take on anything else.' He ran his fingers down the length of her arms and then let her go. 'Joanna, I'm tired of all this secrecy. I want us to be out in the open, living together as husband and wife.' The corners of his mouth turned in and then he said softly, 'Isn't that what you want, too?'

Their eyes met for a long moment. 'You know it is, Matt.'

'Then let's set a date.' Enthusiasm lent lightness to his voice. 'We don't want a big fuss, do we?'

'No.' Joanna pretended to shudder. 'I've done all that.'

Matt looked relieved. 'Me, too. So when and where?'

Just like that. Joanna felt a curl of resentment. 'I can't make a snap decision like that. I'll have to talk to Jason and—'

A frown etched itself between Matt's eyebrows. 'I haven't liked to push but he's OK about us now, isn't he?'

'I haven't told him.' Her voice had got smaller.

'Oh, Joanna…' Matt's eyes clouded with disbelief and disappointment.

'I know.' She bit her lip. 'I said I would but it's never seemed the right time.'

'Joanna, we love each other.' His voice resonated with husky conviction. 'It's right for us to be married, don't you agree?'

She nodded and swallowed the lump in her throat. 'I'll talk to Jason tonight.'

It had been a while since Joanna had got home first. When the front door slammed and Jason's schoolbag hit the floor, the nerves in her tummy tightened like fine wires.

'Mum? You home?'

'Got an early mark.' She manufactured a quick smile when he clattered into the kitchen.

'Thought you might have got the sack.' His mouth tipped into a teasing grin. Opening the fridge door, he helped himself to a carton of flavoured milk.

'Not a chance.' Joanna closed the oven door and set the timer. 'Seeing I'm home early, I thought we'd have a roast.'

'Cool. I'll just get out of my clobber.' Taking his milk, he shot through the door into the hallway.

I have to tell him. The mantra kept going round and round in Joanna's head as she rolled pastry for an apple pie for dessert.

And she'd had plenty of chances, she fretted later.

For some reason her son had been following her around like a puppy—into the laundry while she ran through a load of washing, out into the back garden when she'd pegged it on the line. Now, as she bent over their little veg patch to gather some rosemary to go with the roast potatoes, he was there again.

She sent him a quizzical half-smile. 'Do I look like I'm about to faint?'

'Sorry?'

'You've been hovering like you're waiting to catch me or something… That should do it.' She folded the sprigs of rosemary into the palm of her hand, plucking off several leaves of basil for good measure.

'Uh, I need to run something past you, Jo…' he said awkwardly. 'It's kind of important.'

Joanna ignored the kick in her heart rate. Was he in some kind of trouble? Play it cool, she warned herself silently. 'Come and talk to me, then, while I get the veg ready,' she said, buying time. 'I thought we'd have new potatoes and rosemary, baby carrots and greens of some kind, OK?'

Jason grunted a non-reply.

Joanna set to work at the island bench in the kitchen, feeling her stomach churning beyond belief as Jason determinedly dragged up a high stool and sat opposite her.

'I want to go back to Canberra to live, Mum.'

Joanna's mind emptied. Whatever she'd half feared, it hadn't been this. She forced herself to breathe slowly. 'Aren't you happy here?'

The boy lifted a shoulder. 'I want to go back to my old school. I'll have a better chance of getting into the AIS from there. There'll be special tours through the institute during the term and stuff happening all the time. I'll get to know the ropes beforehand and I'll meet coaches who can help me.'

Oh, lord, he was deadly serious. Joanna stared blankly at the potato she'd begun peeling. And where did that leave her? Separated from Matt until Jason finished his schooling and become established at the institute? She felt her insides hollow out. She was going to have to choose again. And every instinct was screaming it would *have* to be Jason over Matt.

She could have wept at the injustice of it all. She couldn't expect Matt to up stakes and follow her to Canberra. Not when he was only just getting the sports-medicine clinic up and running. He'd lose financially and no one could afford to do that in today's economic conditions.

'Come on, Jo...' Jason cajoled, giving her an upside-down grin. 'It won't be the end of the world.'

Not for him, perhaps. *But what about me?* Almost mechanically, she brushed the potatoes with olive oil and placed them into the roasting pan. 'I suppose I could try to get my old job back at the Canberra Medical Centre.' She said it without too much conviction.

Jason looked startled. 'Why would you want to do that?'

'Because...' Joanna licked her lips and stared at him. 'Because I'm your mother and I couldn't—I mean, you can't go off and live on your own.'

'I wouldn't be on my own!' Jason laughed in disbelief, looking as though the weight of the world had just dropped off his young shoulders. 'I'd live with Nana and Grandad Winters. I already talked to Grandad about it on that weekend in Sydney.'

'And you didn't think to talk to me?' Joanna's relief that she wouldn't have to be parted from Matt was lost in her hurt.

'I'm old enough to take responsibility for myself,' he said with youthful brashness. 'I don't expect you to come with me. I know you've got a life here—with Matt. You want to be with him, don't you?' he said after a minute.

Joanna swallowed the sudden lump in her throat. 'He's…asked me to marry him and I've said yes…'

Jason went quite still and then something quite incredible happened in the backs of his eyes. 'That's terrific,' he said softly. 'Matt's a good guy.'

Joanna blinked the sudden wetness away from her eyes. 'And you don't mind?'

'No.' Jason looked amused. 'I'm not a kid. I guessed what was going on. And that night Matt was here after the sports meet—he knew where everything was in the kitchen. He never missed a beat. I'd have to be a moron not to know he'd been here with you.'

'Oh…' Joanna felt the heat in her cheeks. 'Well, yes, he has, but only once or twice.'

'Mum.' Jason reached across the pan of potatoes and patted her wrist. 'It's OK.'

'Really?'

He rolled his eyes. 'As Steffi would say, it's fab.' And to show he was really grown up, he added, 'I'll give Matt a call now and ask him to come for dinner, shall I?'

'Oh.' Joanna put a hand to her trembling mouth. 'I'll need to do more potatoes, then.'

They made the meal an occasion, setting the silky oak table in the dining room with the best linen, china and cutlery. And Matt brought roses, exquisite just-opening blooms of the most delicate apricot with a pearly sheen, which Joanna declared simply had to go on the dinner table.

The roast was superb and Matt carved it with surgical precision. And they had several toasts with a lovely unwooded Chardonnay from Joanna's little cellar.

'I should have a present for you guys.' Rather overcome with sentiment, Jason swallowed hard.

Matt's eyes sparked a brilliant blue. 'You've given us the only present we wanted, mate—to allow us all to become a family.'

Jason's ears turned pink and he mumbled something unintelligible. Joanna, empathising with his teenage embarrassment, announced it was time for dessert. The pie was warm, deep and full of crunchy apple, the pastry rich and sweet. She served it with ice cream and watched the two men in her life scoop it up with obvious enjoyment.

Over coffee and some rich, dark after-dinner mints, which Joanna had been keeping for a special occasion, she said thoughtfully, 'Are you sure you're OK about living with Nana and Grandad Winters, Jase?'

He snorted a laugh. 'Nana will spoil me rotten. And I won't get in the way,' he promised with his new-found maturity. 'Some weekends I'll go out to Nan and Pop Davidson.'

'They're my parents.' Joanna turned to enlighten Matt.

He nodded and looked from his bride-to-be to his future stepson. 'And you'll both have to meet *my* parents, Hugh and Margo. My dad is a mad keen rugby fan, Jason. I'd guess he'll be interested to chat about your dad.'

Jason nodded and caught his lip, looking as though everything, although it was wonderful, was happening a bit too fast to take in. In a flurry of arms and legs he got up from the table, offering, 'I'll wash up if you guys want to start making plans and stuff.'

It was late when Matt left but the light was still on in Jason's bedroom. Seeing it, Joanna tapped on the door and went in.

'Can't sleep?'

'Just reading.' Throwing his magazine to one side, he raised his arms and stretched. 'You OK?'

She nodded. 'Matt and I have discussed wedding dates and things.' Joanna dropped onto the edge of the bed beside him. 'We thought a month from next Saturday. That'll bring us into spring. And we both like the idea of a church wedding but nothing grand, so we've decided the Grove chapel might be the way to go. It's non-denominational so that doesn't put pressure on anyone.'

Jason buried his chin in his upturned hand. 'Are you going to wear bride stuff?'

'Oh, please!' Joanna chuckled and rolled her eyes. 'Both Matt and I have been married before so this time around what we pledge to each other will seem more important than what we wear.'

'Matt's been married?' Jason jerked his knees up to his chin.

'Mmm.' Joanna looked down, fingering the soft weave of the bedspread. 'His wife was killed. She was pregnant at the time. Matt's little boy survived only a few hours...'

A beat of silence.

'That must have been rough.'

'Yes. Matt was left with nothing.' After a pause, she said quietly, 'I was much more fortunate. Even though I lost your dad, I had you to remember him by.' She blinked a bit. 'I'm going to miss you, Jase...'

'Yeah. I know, Mum.' The boy's voice was gruff. 'I'll miss you too. But I need to do this. Anyway...' he lifted a shoulder '...it's not for a few months yet.'

Joanna took a deep, steadying breath. 'You'll come home for holidays, won't you?'

Jason grinned. 'Sure. And I'm hoping you and Matt will come to me. We could go down to the snow country like we used to.'

'That sounds like a good plan,' Joanna said slowly. 'But I don't know whether Matt can ski.'

'He can.' Jason blocked a yawn and reached over to switch off his bedside lamp. 'I already asked him.'

Of course he had. ''Night, then.' There was a smile in Joanna's voice as she leant across and ruffled his hair.

''Night.'

'See you in the morning.' Levering herself up from the edge of the bed, she moved quietly to the door.

'Mum?'

Joanna paused with her hand on the doorknob. 'Yes, love?'

'Are you and Matt planning to have kids?'

The unexpectedness of the question sent Joanna blank for a second. 'Ah...yes. We'd like to.' She bit her lip. 'Would you mind?'

'Nah—be good...' Jason's voice was already blurred with sleep.

'Don't you dare go hiring a restaurant!' Deb Carlisle upended a pan of muffins onto a wire rack to cool.

She'd invited Joanna to Featherdale for morning tea. 'We'll have the reception here.'

'But, Deb...' Joanna poured boiling water into the teapot '...you've enough on your plate.'

'Joanna, I want to do this for you and Matt. Please, let me.'

Joanna opened her mouth and shut it. When Deb had her teeth into something, it seemed easier to go with the flow. Besides, she knew their wedding reception, left in her future sister-in-law's capable hands, would be wonderful. 'OK, then, thank you.' Joanna brought the teapot to the table. 'It's awfully generous of you.'

'Rats!' Deb flapped a hand. 'I'll love every minute of it. Come on, now. Let's have our tea and you can fill me in on all the details. I know it's at the chapel. My darling brother told me that much. Is your dad giving you away?'

'No.' Joanna bit into one of the warm muffins. 'I hate that expression anyway. The aisle in the chapel is only short so Jason is going to walk me to meet Matt at the altar.'

'Oh...' Deb's eyes misted over. 'How lovely. What else?'

'Well, Matt and I were hoping you and Scott would be our witnesses.'

'Oh, we'd love to! Scott's arm's come ahead in leaps and bounds. He's managing to do quite a bit now. What are you wearing?' Deb leapfrogged onto the next question.

Joanna stirred her tea thoughtfully. 'Well, it's an afternoon ceremony so I thought something elegant but not too bridal.'

'Oh…' Deb's face fell. 'Why not? You'd look gorgeous as a bride.'

'No, Deb.' Joanna held up her hands. 'Definitely not. But I'll make a nice compromise, I promise.'

Deb had to be content with that. 'How many are you and Matt asking? I'll need to know for the catering.'

'About thirty. I'll give you firm numbers as soon as I can. But there'll just be our folk from the clinic, a few friends, your boys, of course, and the three sets of grandparents.'

Deb chuckled. 'We're going to be quite an extended family soon, aren't we?'

Joanna suppressed a shiver, realising how close they'd come to not being a family at all. She bit down on her bottom lip. 'You know, Deb, if you hadn't said anything to me that day…'

'Joanna, you and Matt would have found your way,' Deb reinforced softly. 'True love always does. Haven't you noticed?'

CHAPTER ELEVEN

MATT had thought their wedding day would never come. Yet here it was and he felt as nervous as a cat on a high wire. 'Got the ring?' he asked Scott for the umpteenth time.

Scott sent his eyes heavenwards and tapped the inside pocket of his jacket. 'Stop worrying, mate,' he joked. 'You'll be hitched soon enough.'

Matt blew out a hard breath. He couldn't wait. He wanted his ring on Joanna's finger, something tangible that would shout to the world the beginning of their lives together.

A faintly mysterious smile played around his mouth. He had a surprise for her. She'd vetoed an engagement ring as such so he'd suggested they have a special wedding ring made instead. Joanna had been happy to go along with that, and apart from having her finger sized at the jeweller's she'd left the choosing of the ring to Matt.

And she was going to love it. He'd pored over various designs with the jeweller, finally deciding on a simple band of gold. But what set the ring apart and made it unique were the four beautiful Argyle diamonds, their rose-tinted brilliance enhanced even further by the rubbed-over Victorian setting.

Matt couldn't wait to place it on his bride's finger.

* * *

Joanna looked in the cheval mirror, a little amazed at her reflection. She'd wanted to look beautiful for Matt and, not to put too fine a point on it, she thought she'd achieved nearly that.

Oh, lord. She took a fractured breath and wondered if it was possible to overdose on sheer happiness. And her dress was just right. In ivory silk with a slim-line skirt, it flowed gently around her ankles, the narrow beaded straps across the shoulders giving an elegant touch to the otherwise simple design.

Joanna did a little twirl this way and that in front of the mirror. There was no way of denying it. And she realised she didn't want to anyway. She looked bridal.

The atmosphere in the chapel was hushed. Word had gone round that the bride had arrived. Matt's throat worked as he swallowed and moved to take his place with Scott in front of the altar.

Joanna paused at the entrance to the chapel, her hand securely tucked in her son's arm. Jason turned and winked. 'You look fab, Mum,' he murmured.

She squeezed his arm and took a steadying breath, for a second looking around her. Feathers of late afternoon sunshine were just beginning to filter through the stained-glass windows at the rear of the altar. And the ancient silky-oak pews looked as though they'd been especially polished for the occasion.

She took her gaze higher, seeing the light from the old-fashioned chandelier spilling down, shimmering like weightless water so that it appeared to illuminate the warmth in the faces that were turned expectantly towards them.

With a youthful grin, Jason nudged her back to reality. 'Matt's waiting,' he reminded her. 'Hadn't we better get a move on?'

The wedding reception was in full swing, the buzz of conversation interspersed with shards of laughter filling the night air.

'It's lovely we were able to hold everything outdoors, isn't it?' Joanna smiled at her husband, his body warm against hers as they rocked gently together on the impromptu dance floor.

'Mmm.' Matt kissed her lingeringly.

'I love my ring.' Joanna lifted her hand from his shoulder, watching as the outdoor lighting caught the sparkle.

'Thought you would.' There was a boyish grin on Matt's face. 'I had to work lots of overtime to afford it. But I didn't mind.'

'I should hope not...'

'We had to have diamonds anyway.'

'Tell me why.' Joanna smiled, indulging him.

'Because they're for ever.' His eyes glittered briefly. 'And that, my love, is what we're all about.'

'Oh, Matt...' She blinked away a mist of tears and hugged him tighter.

'Ah, there you are!' Deb bore down on them. 'Sorry to interrupt but you have to cut the wedding cake.'

'Now?' Matt looked pained.

'Now!' His twin tugged him by the arm. 'Bring your wife and let's have you over here at the round table. It can't wait, it's an ice-cream cake.'

'Whose idea was this?' Matt grumbled gently, as they trundled across the lawn to more applause.

'The ice-cream cake?' Tucked close to his side, Joanna laughed with delight at what she saw. 'I think we need look no further than my son and your nephews. Look at them, holding out their plates and practically drooling.'

'Disgusting.' Matt shook his head but Joanna heard him chuckle as they took up the beribboned knife and with his hand on hers plunged it into the rich, creamy confection.

'Have we mingled enough, do you think?' They were lingering over their coffee and, tucked away in the shelter of the old Moreton Bay fig tree, they could have been the only two people in the world.

'More than enough, I'd say.' Matt trapped her hand against his chest. 'Reckon we could just sneak away?'

'No.' Joanna was firm. 'Not when everyone's come to wish us well, and some from long distances, too.'

'Knew you'd say that.' Matt kissed her hand on the way to his lap. 'Happy?'

For answer, she rubbed her cheek against his shoulder. 'But perhaps you're right—we should make a move. And soon.'

'Really?' His smile was as old as time.

'Mmm.' She leant against him, glorying in the solid strength of his body.

'Shall we try for a baby soon?' Matt's arms were around her waist, pulling her back against him. He so wanted her.

Joanna felt the heat of desire ripple through her body. She loved him so much. Turning her face to his, she pressed light kisses on his mouth, once, twice, three times. 'Are twins catching, do you suppose?'

A chuckle rose in his chest. 'You're the doctor, you tell me.'

'Perhaps they take twice as long to make. What do you think?'

His head rested against hers and the soft sigh of his breath teased her hair. 'I think we should say our farewells and make tracks out of here.'

In a time-honoured ritual, the guests formed a circle while the bridal couple began moving in opposite directions, kissing and hugging their way around the circle, until they met up again where they'd begun.

Joanna, smiling a bit unsteadily, made a quick twirl and sent her bouquet flying.

Steffi screamed, letting go of Kim's hand just long enough to catch it. Putting her cheek to the lush blooms, she looked across at the newly-weds. 'I just love happy endings,' she sighed dreamily.

Laughing, Matt and Joanna linked hands, and with a final wave to their families and friends they ducked through the circle and fled into the moonlight.

Modern Romance™
...seduction and
passion guaranteed

Tender Romance™
...love affairs that
last a lifetime

Sensual Romance™
...sassy, sexy and
seductive

Blaze Romance™
...the temperature's
rising

Medical Romance™
...medical drama on
the pulse

Historical Romance™
...rich, vivid and
passionate

27 new titles every month.

*With all kinds of Romance for
every kind of mood...*

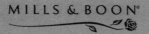

Medical Romance™

THE DOCTOR'S DESTINY by Meredith Webber

Dr Rory Forrester thought he knew better than
Nurse Alana Wright – yet she found him incredibly
attractive! They might be colleagues in conflict, but
the chemistry between them was intense. Rory
realised he had found an angel who could answer his
prayers – but one thing stood in their way...

THE SURGEON'S PROPOSAL by Lilian Darcy

Theatre sister Annabelle Drew was shattered when
one of her guests uttered 'Stop the wedding' as she
was about to say 'I do'! But surgeon Dylan Calford
had no regrets – until he discovered how badly
Annabelle had needed her marriage of convenience.
So he proposed that he should be her groom instead...

UNDER SPECIAL CARE by Laura MacDonald

Mutual attraction flared between Sister Louise Keating
and Dr Matt Forrester, and a whirlwind marriage
followed. But finding time for each other proved
impossible, and they separated. Now, a year on,
they're working together again, in the special care
baby unit. As they heal their tiny patients, can they
also heal their marriage...?

On sale 7th March 2003

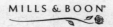

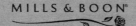

MILLS & BOON®

THE

Regency

RAKES

A wonderful 6 book
Regency series

2 Glittering Romances
in each volume

**Volume 6 on sale from
7th March 2003**

FREE!

2 Books
and a surprise gift!

We would like to take this opportunity to thank you for reading this Mills & Boon® book by offering you the chance to take TWO more specially selected titles from the Medical Romance™ series absolutely FREE! We're also making this offer to introduce you to the benefits of the Reader Service™—

- ★ FREE home delivery
- ★ FREE gifts and competitions
- ★ FREE monthly Newsletter
- ★ Books available before they're in the shops
- ★ Exclusive Reader Service discount

Accepting these FREE books and gift places you under no obligation to buy; you may cancel at any time, even after receiving your free shipment. Simply complete your details below and return the entire page to the address below. **You don't even need a stamp!**

YES! Please send me 2 free Medical Romance books and a surprise gift. I understand that unless you hear from me, I will receive 4 superb new titles every month for just £2.55 each, postage and packing free. I am under no obligation to purchase any books and may cancel my subscription at any time. The free books and gift will be mine to keep in any case.

M3ZEB

Ms/Mrs/Miss/Mr ....Initials..
BLOCK CAPITALS PLEASE

Surname...

Address...

....

....Postcode ....

Send this whole page to:
UK: The Reader Service, FREEPOST CN81, Croydon, CR9 3WZ
EIRE: The Reader Service, PO Box 4546, Kilcock, County Kildare (stamp required)